SUMMER ROSE

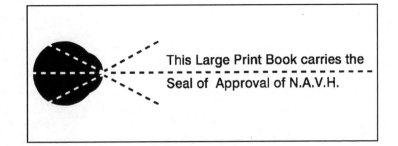

This Large Print Book carries the
Seal of Approval of N.A.V.H.

SUMMER ROSE

ELIZABETH SINCLAIR

THORNDIKE PRESS
A part of Gale, Cengage Learning

GALE
CENGAGE Learning·

Detroit • New York • San Francisco • New Haven, Conn • Waterville, Maine • London

GALE
CENGAGE Learning®

LIBRARY OF CONGRESS CATALOGING-IN-PUBLICATION DATA

Sinclair, Elizabeth.
 Summer rose / by Elizabeth Sinclair. — Large print ed.
  p. cm. — (Hawks mountain series; bk. 2) (Thorndike Press large print clean reads)
  ISBN 978-1-4104-4791-3 (hardcover) — ISBN 1-4104-4791-X (hardcover)
 1. Large type books. 2. Women—Southern States—Fiction. 3. West Virginia—Fiction. 4. Domestic fiction. I. Title.
PS3619.I5478S866 2012
811'.6—dc23   2012015045

Published in 2012 by arrangement with BelleBooks, Inc.

Printed in the United States of America
1 2 3 4 5 6 7 16 15 14 13 12

DEDICATION

This book is dedicated to the people in my life who love animals as much as I do: my son, Bobby; his girlfriend, Jennie Koch; my friend Kellie Sharpe; my editor, Deb Smith and my husband, Bob. There's a special place in heaven for all of you.

Granny Jo's Journal

SUMMER

Hi, ya'all,

So you took my advice and came back to our little town for another visit. But even if it's your first visit to Carson, you're not gonna be disappointed. Now that the temperatures have heated up, it seems things around town are doing likewise.

George Collins, Carson's windbag mayor, is harassing Doc Mackenzie about all the wild animals he has out at the Paws and Claws Animal Clinic and Wildlife Sanctuary. George says they're a danger to the community. Doc says George has bees in his bonnet, and there's nothing dangerous about any of his animals. Can't convince the darn fool mayor that they're just babies, and they're not gonna hurt a soul. Doc's holding his ground, but if George has his way, Doc will have to get rid of them. Personally, I think it has a lot to do with Davy, George's boy, working at the sanctuary.

Rumor has it that Doc's new assistant and Davy have something up their sleeves, but no one knows what it is, not even Laureene Talbot, which is a minor miracle considering there's nothing in this town that old busybody doesn't get wind of. Guess we'll all have to wait and see.

Becky and Nick's wedding plans are in full swing and should be ready to go right on time for their late summer wedding. Last I heard Becky's ordered daisies for the entire wedding: church, bouquets and all. She says there's something special about them little white flowers that means something to her and Nick. Won't say what. Her and Nick just smile and kiss whenever I ask.

There's a new gal working at the social services office with Becky. Name's Amantha James. Goes by Mandy. My Becky says she's a real go-getter and has a plan for the school that's gonna turn a few heads. But that's a tale for another day.

The house that Jonathan Prince fella is building outside town is really coming along. It's gonna be a big one, too. A mansion, some say. One of the young men Nick's training to be an EMT works for the construction company building it, and he says, outside of the big hotels in Charleston, he's never seen anything this size before.

Well, I have to go now. It's time for Lydia Collins' radio show, and I never miss it. After that, I'm off to Charleston with Becky to have lunch at one of those big, fancy restaurants, and then we're gonna pick out her wedding gown. But don't you go away. I have a feeling things around Carson are going to get real interesting, real fast, and you won't want to miss a minute of it.

Love,
Granny Jo

CHAPTER 1

She took one look at him and gagged.

The reaction of the stunning, auburn-haired woman, who'd just entered the Paws & Claws Animal Clinic and Wildlife Sanctuary, surprised Dr. Hunter Mackenzie. He'd never thought of himself as particularly handsome, but he wasn't *that* bad either.

As he stared at her, she clamped one hand over her mouth and pressed the other one to her flat stomach. She closed her startlingly blue eyes and swallowed repeatedly.

Deciding her reaction had been physical and no fault of his, he pressed the telephone's mouthpiece, into which he'd been talking when she'd entered the clinic, against his shoulder. "Are you all right?"

Swallowing one last time, she coughed lightly, and then removed her hand from her mouth. "I'm fine. I think I may have eaten something for lunch that didn't agree with me."

11

He studied her for a moment. "Are you sure?" Though her face remained pale and drawn, she smiled wanly and nodded. To be certain, he waited a moment before going back to his phone call. He motioned toward the waiting area at the side of the room. "Why don't you have a seat while I finish my phone call?"

She nodded and walked to the grouping of plastic chairs lining the clinic's waiting room.

Hunter's alert and decidedly appreciative gaze followed her shapely form across the waiting room, noting almost absently that she had no animals with her. Once she'd safely seated herself, he removed the phone's receiver from his shoulder. With a sigh of resignation, he went back to his conversation with the mayor of Carson, West Virginia, George Collins.

"George, none of the sanctuary's animals have ever escaped or attacked any of the townspeople. What keeps making the council think they're a safety risk?" Stupid question. Hunter knew who kept the belief alive. Since he'd become mayor of Carson, Collins had launched a ridiculous crusade to shut down the sanctuary. Hunter would make book on it that George had browbeaten the council members into agreeing with him.

The odd part was that Hunter had no idea why George was so hell-bent to shut it down.

"Listen, Mackenzie, we know you took in an African lion the other day. We can't have that kind of threat living on the edge of a populated community." Collins' voice boomed from the phone into Hunter's ear.

The frustration building inside Hunter threatened to overwhelm him. He took a deep breath, and then leaned forward, planting his forearms solidly on the desk. "Good grief, George, why don't you people call me before you get yourselves all in a lather? The lion is a cub, orphaned when its mother died. He's just a few weeks old. It'll be quite a while before he poses a risk to the town or anyone in it. By then, I'll have found a zoo that will take him."

"The cub will soon be gone, but that doesn't solve the problem of the other animals you keep out there and the ones that will inevitably replace the cub." The mayor's voice gained volume again. "They're wild, too, and dangerous. They . . ."

While Mayor Collins again listed all the reasons for closing the sanctuary, arguments Hunter had heard every time he obtained a new animal, he assessed his female visitor.

She busied herself by leafing through a magazine she'd found on the side table. Unfortunately, because of her bent head, a thick curtain of auburn hair obscured her face from his view. As if she'd heard his thoughts, she swept back her shoulder-length hair and tucked it behind her ear. The color had begun to return to her cheeks, and he noted that her skin had a peaches and cream quality that he'd only read about in books.

"Mackenzie, do you hear me?"

George's irate voice blasting into Hunter's ear pulled him abruptly from the pleasurable view. He sighed and dragged his attention back to his tormentor. "Yes, I hear you. What I'm not hearing are any new arguments to convince me to close down the sanctuary. I don't know how many ways I can say this, but those animals are not dangerous. Most of them are babies who've lost their mothers, either naturally or with the help of some fool with a gun. The others are sick or injured and in no shape to hurt anyone." Hunter took a deep breath and repeated the words he'd been saying to George for six months now. "I will not shut down the sanctuary because a few people think a bunch of baby animals are going to sneak out in the middle of the night and eat them."

"You're a pigheaded man, Hunter Mackenzie, but this is not the end of this."

Click!

The line went dead. Hunter stared down at the humming phone. "I'm sure it's not." He shook his head, and then placed the receiver in the cradle.

"Problems?"

Her soft voice drew his attention. "Nothing I haven't heard before." He relaxed and folded his hands on the desk. "Sorry to keep you waiting. I'm afraid my assistant picked this week to elope, and I'm trying to be vet, receptionist and assistant."

She stood, and then came to stand before him. Straightening her back, she reached in her large, black tote bag, pulled out a folded newspaper and then laid it on the desk in front of him.

"I want to apply for the job you advertised in the want ads."

The ad he'd placed two days ago in the *Hawks Mountain Herald* glared back at him from inside a thick circle of red ink.

She stuck out her hand. "Rose Hamilton."

He grasped it and had to pause before speaking. The odd sensation of warm water swamping him from head to toe then sucking him beneath its surface came over him.

The tension fostered by the mayor's phone call ebbed away as if it had never existed. Hunter hung onto her hand overlong, enjoying the total peace her touch had brought to him.

From beyond the wall behind him, a dog barked and soon a cacophonous chorus of *woofs* and *yips* could be heard.

Hunter shook himself free of the residual effects of her touch, released her hand, and then stood.

"Hunter Mackenzie," he said loud enough to be heard above the racket. He smiled apologetically. "Excuse me." Stepping back, and with a balled fist, he hit the wall once. The dogs quieted, except for a few stray *yips* that quickly died away. "Normally, that doesn't bother me, but I'm not up to that noise right now. That phone call managed to produce the start of a headache." He rubbed a forefinger on the side of his temple.

"Stress." She flashed a radiant smile at him. Suddenly, the sunshine illuminating the room seemed to brighten considerably. "I'm a nurse. A licensed practical nurse."

He continued to stare, mostly at her full lips. He tore his gaze away. Reaching into her voluminous tote bag, she extracted her wallet. Taking a small white card from her billfold, she handed it to him.

Finally able to rouse himself from his uncharacteristic fascination with the shape and color of her eyes, he coughed and scanned the card that verified her nursing credentials. "So, you want the job as my assistant? And you think nursing sick humans qualifies you to nurse sick animals?"

"Dr. Mackenzi—"

"Hunter." He motioned for her to take the seat facing the desk, and then passed the card back to her.

"Hunter," Rose went on, her heart beating a wild tattoo against her chest. She took the seat, grateful to get off her shaking legs, and prayed silently to find the right words to convince him to give her the job. "Nursing is nursing, be it with animals or humans. They all need the same care, the same attention and the same compassion."

He smiled again, and she felt something inside her drop to the bottom of her stomach. *Oh, no.* She couldn't be sick again. *Not now.* When he looked away for a second, she realized the sensation she'd just felt had nothing to do with her stomach upset, and everything to do with the man smiling at her.

"I can't argue that point, Ms. Hamilton."

"Rose."

"Rose," he repeated, then licked his lips as if tasting the sound of her name. Her stomach flipped. "Did you bring a résumé?"

Once more she delved into her tote. This time, she pulled out the folder she'd tucked in there that morning before leaving the motel. Handing it to him, she said, "I think you'll find everything you need in here."

While he scanned her work record, Rose assessed the doctor. Age? About thirty-four or thirty-five. Laugh lines around his hazel eyes and mouth. A good sense of humor? His immaculate lab coat told her he believed in a clean, antiseptic working environment. The open-necked, white-and-blue-striped shirt beneath the lab coat could mean a casual, relaxed personality. His brown hair showed attempts at waving despite the smooth comb he'd given it.

Then, to her surprise, her perusal shifted, became less impersonal. Shoulders wide enough to support another man, or a woman with some heavy burdens to carry. Full lips and an expressive mouth. Good kisser?

Acutely aware that she had just trespassed into dangerous territory, Rose stopped the inventory abruptly.

"Your résumé is quite impressive." He handed the folder back to her. "Why aren't you looking for a job in a hospital?"

She had anticipated this question. Replacing the folder in her tote, Rose stalled for time while she silently rehearsed her carefully prepared answer.

Finally confident, she looked him in the eye. "Because, when I came to Carson, I found it to be exactly the type of town I'd love to settle down in. Unfortunately, you don't have a hospital, and I don't want to commute. Besides, my car is far from reliable, and I can't afford a new one right now. I'm afraid I'm not trained to do anything else, so working as your assistant is the closest I could come in Carson to finding a job in my field of work." '

She said a silent prayer that her explanation sounded as convincing now as it had when she'd composed it before the motel's bathroom mirror that morning.

The vet stared at her for a long moment. Was that skepticism she saw in his expression or just her imagination? She really hated subterfuge, but if he knew the truth, he might not hire her, and she *needed* this job.

Rose had been about to add that she'd grown up in a small town, when the door opened. A young boy of about ten careened into the room. His freckled face glowed with a heated flush, and his midnight-black hair shot out in all directions. Through the open door behind him, Rose could see a dusty, red bike lying on its side, the front wheel still spinning.

"Whose car is that?" The boy pointed toward the parking lot.

"Mine," Rose said.

"Boy, it's sure a wreck."

She certainly didn't need that to be pointed out. The car had been on the verge of dying for weeks now, and she'd prayed it would hold out for just a bit longer. Just until she got a job and could get it fixed. Rather than explaining all this to the boy, she just smiled.

He turned to Hunter. "My mom said you have a lion cub. Can I see him?"

"And hello to you, too." Hunter smiled at the young boy. "Rose, this is Davy Collins, the mayor's son, who normally has very good manners."

"Sorry." The boy dipped his head, and then looked at Rose from beneath his long, black lashes. "Hello, ma'am. Nice to meet ya."

Social obligations seen to, Davy swept past Rose. She got a whiff of fresh air, sunshine, and something chocolate flavored that she assumed came from the candy bar protruding from his back pocket.

"Can I see the cub now, Doc? Huh?" His young face transmitted the urgency of his request.

"I don't know, Davy. Your dad would skin me alive if he knew I let you near that animal."

The boy frowned. "I won't tell him. Beside, since he and my mom got divorced, he doesn't care about me anyway." The brightness in the boy's eyes dimmed a fraction.

Hunter frowned. "Davy, as long as he lives, your dad will care about you."

Davy shrugged.

Hunter drummed the eraser end of a pencil on the desktop. Rose got the feeling Hunter wanted to say more, but didn't. "Does your mom know you're here?"

"Yup. She said I could come over as long as I didn't get too close to the animals and didn't get in your way. Now, can I go see the cub?" His scuffed sneakers shuffled on the spotlessly clean linoleum, as if they had a brain of their own and couldn't wait to be off to this new adventure.

Hunter glanced at Rose. "I'm kind of busy right now, and you can't go alone. You'll have to wait."

"Aw, Doc."

Rose winked at Davy, then looked at Hunter and smiled. "If it's okay, I'd like to see the lion cub, too." Rose stood and moved to stand beside Davy. "Why don't you show both of us, and that way you won't have to worry about Davy."

Hunter couldn't believe the impact of that smile on his equilibrium. If she'd requested he set fire to himself, he wasn't sure he could have refused her. "No fair. That's two against one." He looked from one to the other. "Okay, we'll go see the cub." He activated the answering machine, stood, and then circled the desk. Stopping Davy's plunge for the door with a hand on the boy's slim shoulder, Hunter looked down at him. "You have to do exactly as I say. The cub may be little, but his claws are still dangerous. Deal?"

Davy looked up at Hunter with pure love and admiration shining from his dark brown eyes. "Deal." He held up his hand, the palm stained with chocolate candy. "Promise."

The three of them left the office and walked toward a large, fenced-in enclosure several hundred yards from the office. On the way, they skirted Rose's less-than-reliable old Taurus, and then passed a very small, but lovely house with a wide front porch and a two-story garage.

"Yours?" Rose asked.

Hunter nodded. "I wanted to live close by. I'm the kind of guy who likes to roll out of bed, grab a cup of coffee, and then roll into the front door of my work place."

She laughed. "I know just what you mean. I'm not a morning person either."

Almost immediately, Hunter's mind launched into a vision of what Rose would look like in the morning, sleep still in her eyes, pillowcase creases on her face and her auburn hair splayed out across his bare chest.

Whoa! You're getting yourself in way over your head, fella. Remember, you're the guy who doesn't want anything to do with the responsibilities that relationships inevitably demand.

How could he have forgotten all the years of raising his siblings, worrying about them, arranging his life around them?

By the time he had his wayward imagination under control, they'd arrived outside a small, cinder block building with a sign over the door with the words *Animal Nursery* emblazoned on a small sign to the side of the door. He opened the door for them and waited while Davy passed through, followed by Rose.

Rose looked around, the nurse in her doing a clinical assessment of the room. The overly warm room held wire cages in a variety of sizes — some empty, some occupied by a variety of furry babies. In the center stood a stainless steel examination table. One wall held cabinets with glass fronts that displayed an array of medicines and instruments and what looked like a baby scale. The odor of antiseptic permeated the spotless surroundings, reminding Rose of a hospital operating room.

"Here's our newest baby," Hunter said, releasing the catch on one of the cages and scooping out a small ball of fur from inside.

The lion cub, a light tan with dark markings on the ears and head, looking amazingly like a larger version of someone's full-grown house cat, stretched its paws out and yawned. Rose ran a tentative finger over the downy fur. In response, the cub licked her hand, its rough tongue sending shivers over her. An odd, but certainly not repulsive feeling.

"Where's its mother?" she asked, continuing to pet the little cub.

"It's a male. Born in captivity in a privately run, roadside zoo out west. The authorities closed the zoo for cruelty to the animals, and the mother died shortly thereafter from the abuse she'd sustained there. A friend of mine had helped with the animal removal and reassignment of the stock and had the cub sent to me. When he's healthy enough, I'll transfer him to a reputable zoo."

"Does he have a name?" Davy stroked the cub's nose.

"No, I'm afraid I've been too busy to think about names." Hunter turned to the boy. "Would you like to name him, Davy?"

"Really, Doc?"

Hunter nodded. "Really."

Davy's eyes glowed with excitement, and then he became serious. "It has to be a special name. One that fits him." The boy stepped back and studied the baby cat, the expression on his young face reflecting his deep consideration of the name issue.

The cub stretched again and curled up in Hunter's hands. Hunter offered the cub to Rose. At first, never having held an animal before, she hesitated. Then the cub licked her hand again, and that's all it took to make her reach for him. Cradling the small animal close, she moved her body back and forth in a rocking motion. His eyes drifted closed.

"You're a natural," Hunter said. "Maybe you can get him to eat. I haven't been able to get him interested in food since he arrived two days ago. If I don't get some food

25

in him soon, I'm afraid . . ." He shifted his gaze to Davy.

Knowing the consequences of the cub not eating, she gave a slight nod. "I'll give it a try."

Hunter set to work preparing an oversized baby bottle filled with a white liquid, then handed it to Rose. She shifted the cub into the crook of her left arm, as if it were a human baby, and offered him the nipple. At first he sniffed it, and then turned away, but moments later, when she commenced a soft cooing sound, the cub turned back, sucked in the nipple and began devouring the formula.

"Well I'll be damned," Hunter said, under his breath. "You're hired."

His unexpected proclamation almost caused her to drop both the cub and the bottle. "Really? You mean it?"

"Anyone who could get that little fella to eat is qualified in my book."

She'd been about to ask Hunter about job benefits when Davy broke in. "Boomer. We can call him Boomer."

"Boomer?" Hunter looked at the small cub still sucking greedily on the nipple and laughed. "Isn't that name kind of big for such a little guy?"

"Maybe now," Davy explained, his face

serious, "but when he grows up, it'll be perfect."

Hunter looked at Rose, who smiled. "Can't argue with that, can you?" She glanced down at the tiny cub. "Besides, now that he's got the hang of eating, he'll be a bruiser in no time, so you can't pin a sissy name like "Tabby" on him. He'd spend all his time fighting off other lions who make fun of him." She looked at a grinning Davy. "Right?"

Davy nodded enthusiastically.

Hunter grinned, too. "Okay, Boomer it is."

The cub had finally stopped feeding, and Rose noted the look of longing on Davy's face. She stepped forward, then stopped. Glancing at Hunter for his okay and receiving it, she carefully shifted the small, furry body into the boy's waiting arms. They all laughed when Boomer stuck his nose into the opening in Davy's shirt front and immediately fell back to sleep.

"I think he thinks I'm his mom," the boy said, a tinge of red coloring his cheeks.

Watching the boy with the cub gave Hunter an idea. Normally, he steered clear of kids, having had enough of them while raising his sister and brother, but he liked Davy. Besides, a chasm separated standing guard 24/7 over two teenage kids and having Davy around for a few hours every day.

"Davy, how would you like to work part-time for me?"

The boy's head snapped up, and his gaze searched Hunter's. "For real, Doc?"

"Yeah, for real. I'll even pay you."

"Cool," the boy exclaimed, his attention immediately recaptured by the cub.

"You could come out after school and on Saturdays and help me feed and water the animals and clean out their pens. What do you think? Is that something you can handle?"

"You bet I can." Davy's eyes sparkled with excitement.

"You'll need to get your mom's okay."

"I will. I promise. She won't care though. She knows I'm a sucker for animals. Mom says I can charm anything with fur on it, just like Dr. Dolittle." The boy's face flushed pink. "She wishes I'd be as eager to do my chores as I am to take care of the animals." He giggled, dipped his head, and turned a slightly darker shade of pink. "She calls me Dr. Littledo sometimes."

"Well, Dr. Littledo, if your mom calls me tonight and okays it, you can start tomorrow."

The grin on Davy's face widened.

"Thanks, Doc."

As Hunter turned away, he caught Rose looking at him. Her half smile made his stomach flip. Just the type of smile he'd envisioned her having first thing in the morning.

Shaking away his thoughts, he stared back at her. "What?"

She shook her head and her long hair shifted back and forth, caressing her cheeks in a very sexy, unconscious come-on. "You're a nice man, Hunter Mackenzie."

"It's nothing. The kid is as natural at this as you seem to be."

She continued to bathe him in her glorious smile.

Despite his efforts not to read anything into it, her smile made him feel like he'd just won the Nobel Peace Prize.

By the time they got back to the office, an elated Davy had rushed off home to get permission to work for Hunter. That left Rose and Hunter to discuss salary and other aspects of her new job.

Rose had just filled out the job application form, when Hunter's curiosity got the better of him.

"I'm amazed at what you did with that cub. I've tried everything to get him to eat.

Have you worked with animals before, had your own pets?"

Rose dipped her head. Her face disappeared behind that veil of auburn hair. "The closest I have ever come to an animal, domestic or wild, is in books and movies and watching people walk their dogs." She lifted her gaze from the form she'd been filling out. "Foster homes don't allow pets. Out there," she motioned toward the animal nursery, "that's the first time I've ever touched an animal."

He couldn't believe it. She seemed so comfortable handling the cub. "You're telling me you had no pets?"

"Well, I had a cricket once for about a week, and then my foster mother found it and stepped on it. She said crickets eat clothes, and she couldn't afford to buy me new ones, so the cricket had to go."

Hunter, who, along with his siblings, had had every kind of pet from a snake to a pot-bellied pig while they were growing up, couldn't imagine anyone not allowing a child to have some kind of animal, fish, insect or bird as a companion. From the tone of her voice, he sensed that, while it had only been a cricket, her pet's death had left a scar on Rose's life.

"You meant what you said out there,

didn't you?"

Roused by her question, Hunter sought to put meaning to it. "What I said?"

"About hiring me," she explained, handing him the completed application form. "You're not going to just file this and forget about me, are you?"

Forget her? Not in this lifetime. "Oh, you're hired all right. You performed a miracle out there. I want to see if it was a fluke, and the only way I can do that is to hire you." He took the form and laid it atop a pile of papers threatening to cascade to the floor at any minute.

Her large eyes opened wider. "Does that mean I'm on a trial basis?"

He laughed. "No, you are not on a trial basis. The job is permanent for as long as you want it. I will expect you here bright and early at eight o'clock tomorrow morning."

"What about your former assistant? Won't she want her job back when she gets home from her honeymoon?"

"No. She'll be moving to Raleigh where her new husband works, which means I need a permanent replacement, and that would be you."

"Well, then, I'll see you tomorrow at eight." She bathed him in a smile unlike any he'd seen from her so far. "I better be getting home."

"Which is where?" He scanned the form she'd just filled out.

"I left that line blank because I'm still looking for a place. Until I find one, I'm staying at the motel out on Route 6." She stood and began gathering up her things to leave.

"If you're interested, the apartment over the garage is empty. I lived there while the carpenters built my house. You're welcome to it if you want. It's completely furnished, and all you'd need to move in right away are your clothes, food and some linens. It's rent-free and comes with the job. Right now, I'm using it for storage, but if you're willing to stick around for a couple of hours after work tomorrow, we can clean it out."

Although the rent-free part fit right into her financial status, the idea of living so close to a man who could turn her knees to mush with a smile cast serious doubts on her decision. Not to mention that right now, letting a man into her life would not be the smartest move on her part.

"May I think about it?"

"Certainly. It's been vacant for almost three years now. A few days more isn't going to change that."

"Fine. I'll see you tomorrow."

"Tomorrow, eight o'clock," he said and winked. Her stomach flipped.

Rose had almost reached the door when she recalled that she'd forgotten one very important thing. "Are there medical benefits with this job?"

In the act of punching the play button on the blinking answering machine, he paused thoughtfully. "Yes, of course."

"Could I ask what they are?"

He walked to the gray filing cabinets, opened a drawer and rifled through a bunch of folders. "My assistant took care of these things. Let me see if I can . . . Yup, here it is." He pulled a file from the drawer. "This explains everything." He handed her a manila folder marked *Health Insurance.*

She sat again. Taking it with shaky fingers, Rose spread the folder open on her lap. Mentally intoning a silent prayer that she would find what she sought, she began leafing through the pages of the medical insurance policy. Holding her breath and knowing that this would mean whether or not she could accept this job and begin a new life, she carefully scanned each page.

It *had* to be here. She *needed* it to be here.

Finally, when the form she'd been searching for caught her eye, she heaved a sigh of relief. Rose read silently.

Maternity benefits take effect ten months after the initial date of employment.

Her heart sank. Not good news to a woman already two and a half months pregnant with twins.

CHAPTER 2

Rose threw her purse on the motel room bed and collapsed heavily on the edge of the mattress. Sighing with exhaustion, she kicked off her shoes and lay back against the pillows, cursing herself for not being better about saving money before all this happened. The lumps pressing into her back reminded her that this motel did not offer the most posh accommodations. Unfortunately, she couldn't afford anything better.

Lying back, she closed her eyes, knowing she had some critical decisions to make that couldn't be put off. She had accepted a job and been offered a rent-free apartment close enough to the office to walk to work, but the job provided no maternity benefits that she could tap into to cover the birth of the twins. All but certain her supervisor had gotten Rose fired from her last job because of the pregnancy while claiming that Rose's termination had been due to staff downsizing, Rose couldn't take that chance this time with Hunter. The babies would remain her little secret for now.

If, when Rose had decided to be a surrogate for them, Beth and her husband had only taken out medical insurance on Rose and the babies instead of paying as they went, Rose wouldn't be facing this dilemma now. But Beth and Patrick hadn't been any better off financially than Rose, and it had taken every spare buck they had to pay the obstetrician.

Despite the lack of maternity benefits, the job did have its pluses. After holding the lion cub and feeding him, she'd lost all her trepidation about working with the animals and, in fact, she had decided that she'd probably enjoy it. Also, if she took the apartment over the garage, living so close to her job would mean she wouldn't have to worry about getting her car fixed right away. Maybe not having maternity benefits didn't signal the end of the world. Without the cost of car repair bills, gas to travel back and forth to work, and rent, she could save enough to cover a decent portion of her doctor and hospital expenses.

Thoughts of the apartment Hunter had offered her brought to mind her strong and unexpected reaction to the handsome vet.

Could she do it? She already knew Hunter held an unexpected attraction for her, an attraction she didn't need complicating her life. She had enough complications already. Would it be foolish for her to move into his apartment and put herself squarely in temptation's way, or would it be more foolish for her to spend time looking for another job that she'd have to commute to with an unreliable car and an apartment that would require the added expense of paying rent?

She rolled to her stomach, rested her chin on her hands and frowned thoughtfully. Logic told her to take the job and the apartment. It only made sense. After all, a grown woman should be able to control her emotions for eight hours out of every day. Shouldn't she?

She sat up. One of the lumps in the mattress bore into her leg, adding one more reason to her list of reasons for taking Hunter's apartment and the job. Punching the lump down with her balled-up fist, she dreamed of a night's sleep on a bed that didn't feel like Mount Rushmore's rock dump.

Being picky had never been one of her personality traits, but right now, her health had to come before everything else, and getting a solid eight hours of sleep played a major role in keeping her fit for the next six and a half months. She spread her hands over her flat stomach.

"You're my responsibilities now," she told the twin lives growing within her. "Your mom would want me to do what's best for the two of you, and that's what I intend to do."

Rising from the bed, she hauled her suitcases from under it and went to the dresser. A few minutes later, she had all the clothes she'd brought with her packed in two suitcases, except a clean uniform and underwear for tomorrow and her night-clothes. She would move into Hunter's apartment and make it her mission to keep her emotions under control. As for the medical bills . . . though she hated having to resort to it, Medicaid would cover them if need be.

A wave of happiness and relief washed over her. She had a job, a roof over her head and a plan to cover her and the babies' medical expenses. Her life was finally smoothing out and in her control.

From beside the suitcase, she picked up a framed photo of a lovely blonde woman and looked at it for a long time. Beth had been such a big part of Rose's life that she had difficulty believing she would never see her best friend again.

"I miss you, but don't worry, your babies will be okay." And for the first time since the accident that had killed Beth and her husband, Rose almost believed it — almost.

The babies would eat well and be cared for. Right now she could promise no more. After all, when she'd agreed to be Beth's surrogate, Rose had never imagined that she would be the one raising the children — not Beth. Had she known that, as much as she loved her foster sister, she would have never volunteered for the job of carrying Beth's babies.

Rose knew that Beth would have been the perfect mother for the twins. Because she'd known a mother's love and lost her mother to cancer at an early age, she'd always loved kids and wanted them with what almost amounted to desperation.

In Rose's case, however, as a result of her mother's lack of nurturing genes and her desertion of her only child, Rose had always been terrified that she'd follow in her mother's footsteps and, as a result, had never planned on having children.

Putting down the picture, she moved to the mirror over the dresser and gazed at her reflection. Rose had been told over and over by one foster parent or another that she had inherited her mother's hair, eyes and stature. How many times had she heard . . . *You're just like your mother.*

She had no idea how they knew or if they really did know. The indisputable fact remained that her mother had deserted her. That her mother didn't have what it takes to raise a child. Rose had to wonder if her outward appearance had been all she'd inherited from the woman who had given birth to her.

Hunter sat at the receptionist's desk and sipped his second cup of morning coffee while he listened to the angry voice of George Collins emanating from the answering machine. When the *beep* interrupted George's tirade about his son working around all those *dangerous wild animals,* Hunter sighed and hit the rewind button. He'd expected the call, but it still made him want to find George and shake some sense into him.

Hunter had Davy's mother's okay, and she was the parent with legal custody of the boy. But he had neither the time nor the patience for George this morning. Hunter felt . . . keyed up. As if he stood on the verge of a momentous happening in his life. Excitement swirled inside him. He felt edgy and unable to sit still.

He'd felt this way when, at age ten, he'd gotten his first bike for Christmas. A blizzard had kept him from riding it for three days. Each day the anticipation had grown greater and greater until he thought he'd burst.

But that was then, and this was now, and the anticipation he felt could not be appeased with a simple bike ride.

Then he heard the sound of gravel crunching beneath tires, then the cough and backfire of a car coming to a stop, and he knew the cause of his edginess. He'd been waiting for Rose's arrival.

He shook his head, and then combed his fingers through his hair. Not a good sign. Not good at all. He needed an assistant, not a relationship. Relationships led to marriage and marriage led to children. If he caved to his emotions, his life would be altered forever. Lord, help him. He had steered clear of this ever since he left college.

Personal experience had made Hunter all too aware of the demands children put on a man's life. After his parents' deaths, he'd been forced into the role of the head of a household overrun by two younger Mackenzie siblings for over four years. He didn't need or want his quiet life disrupted like

41

that again.

Hold it, Mackenzie. She's coming to work. Nothing more. You're letting your imagination get the best of you. Just calm down and keep everything in perspective, and you'll be fine.

The door opened, and the fact that Rose had put up her hair in a tight knot at the back of her head and donned sage green pants and a flowered smock top helped some. However, he could still feel the stirrings of a disturbingly strong attraction.

"Good morning." Rose smiled, making Hunter wish she were bucktoothed and bald or something equally as unappealing.

"Morning." He tore his gaze away and busied himself with his appointment book. "I don't have any appointments until eleven, so that will give you time to feed Boomer and get acquainted with the office routine." He grabbed a sheet of paper from a pad and began writing furiously. When he'd finished, he handed her the paper. "These are the instructions for preparing Boomer's formula. Everything in the nursery is well marked so you shouldn't have any problems. He'll be fed at eight in the morning, twelve noon and four in the evening. For today, you can take the early feedings, and I'll try doing the evening feeding, but I'd like you here just in case he won't eat for me."

Rose accepted the paper and looked at him questioningly. He didn't blame her for looking a bit confused. He'd been babbling and couldn't seem to stop himself.

"I'll be here. I planned on starting to clean out the apartment you offered over the garage right after work."

His head snapped up. "The garage?"

She frowned. "You did say I could live there, right?"

He shook away the cobwebs draped over his brain that prevented him from having a coherent thought. "Oh. Sure. Right. It's still yours if you want it."

"Thanks, and please, let me know if you change your mind about me paying rent."

"I won't change my mind. The apartment comes as a perk of the job. Besides, I want you close by." He paused and began shifting his feet uncomfortably. "I mean . . ."

Before he could say more, she raised her hand to stop him. "Are you absolutely sure about the rent —"

Hunter frowned. "Look, it hasn't been rented for three years. I haven't missed the money, and I don't expect to start just because I now have a tenant. You'll take care of your own utilities. Other than that, it's yours for as long as you want to live there."

"I appreciate this. You won't be sorry," she added, laying her hand on his sleeve.

Hunter moved his arm away slowly, trying not to seem as though he were running for cover, even if he was. As for not being sorry, he'd invited her to live in his backyard . . . Only time would tell. If the way he felt when she'd touched him and smiled at him meant what he thought it did, *sorry* had already started tugging at his coattails.

The phone rang, and they both reached for it at the same time, their hands entwining on the receiver. He quickly pulled away.

She picked up the phone. "Good morning, Paws and Claws Animal Clinic. How may I help you?"

Hunter didn't have to ask who it was. From the other side of the desk, he could hear George Collins demanding to know who he was speaking to. Casually, Hunter picked up Pansy, the orange, tiger-striped house cat, who had adopted Hunter a few days ago. He held the cat close, reminding himself that she needed to be spayed as soon as he had a free moment.

"This is Dr. Mackenzie's new assistant, Rose Hamilton. How may I help you, Mr. Collins?"

Silence, while she listened. Hunter could no longer hear the mayor's ravings across the room. Rose had already worked her magic on the resident thorn in Hunter's backside. Would she work it on him, too?

"Yes, sir. Yes, I understand. I'm afraid the doctor is busy . . ." She glanced at him and Pansy. ". . . with one of the animals right at the moment. I'll give him your message." She shrugged innocently at Hunter's grin. "Yes, sir. No, I won't forget. I've written it all down. Have a good day, sir." She replaced the receiver. "He wants to speak to you about hiring Davy."

"That's the best end-run I've seen since I played high school football. Thanks. I should have known that hiring his son would have him up in arms and that I'd have to face him on it sooner or later. However, what I don't need today is another go-round with our illustrious mayor." He set Pansy down at his feet. "You better get Boomer fed before my scheduled patients start arriving."

He smiled at Rose. She blinked several times, and then grabbed the paper with the recipe for Boomer's formula written on it, and hurried out the door in the direction of the animal nursery.

Hunter watched her go and waited for his heartbeat to resume normalcy, then he bent over and stroked Pansy's soft coat. "You know what, Pansy? This might be tougher than I first thought it would be."

Later that evening, Rose wiped the beads of sweat from her forehead, and then shifted a large box of Hunter's belongings nearer to the pile that he had been moving from the apartment to store downstairs in the garage. She straightened for a second and looked around. Perfect.

The living room, dining room and kitchen were one big open area. And two smaller rooms would serve perfectly as bedrooms. All in all, the place wasn't too big to care for, but not so small she felt cramped.

The furnishings, all leather and wood, reflected a man's taste, but the addition of some bright-colored throw pillows and lacy curtains would give the room a more feminine appeal. A few plants on the tables and a couple of colorful area rugs on the bare wood floor and it would be a place where any woman would be happy to live.

More importantly, free rent aside, the smaller bedroom close to the main bedroom would be perfect for a nursery for the twins. Thoughts of the babies brought to mind the fact that she hadn't told Hunter about her condition yet. Would he let her go when he found out? The last place she worked had, or at least, she was almost certain they had. It just appeared all too coincidental that shortly after she confided her condition to one of the other nurses, Rose's supervisor had called her into her office and laid her off. At least that's how she had put it, but Rose wasn't stupid. She'd been fired.

She knew she'd have to tell Hunter soon. After all, she wouldn't be able to hide it forever. Hopefully, by then, she'd have proven her worth, and he'd keep her on, despite her pregnancy.

"Please tell me that's the last load," Hunter said, climbing the flight of stairs for the umpteenth time and coming face to face with a new pile of boxes. "Where did all this come from?" He flopped down on the end of the couch and leaned back, exhaling a gust of air. "Woman, you're a slave driver."

"Are we taking a break, Mr. Softie?" She grinned. "You need to spend less time over an examination table and more exercising." Despite her good-natured scolding, she flopped down next to him, grateful for the respite, but not about to admit it.

Only after she sat down did Rose realize that the loveseat forced her into closer proximity to Hunter than was good for her peace of mind. A rock-hard thigh pressed intimately against her leg and had her rethinking her earlier advice to Hunter about needing more exercise. Obviously, not a problem for him, but the feel of his leg along hers definitely presented a problem for her. She shifted as close to the arm of the loveseat as space would allow.

He checked his watch. "It's almost seven o'clock. We've been at this for two hours. I don't know about you, but I missed supper and I'm starved. Let's go down to my place and get something to eat."

The playfulness she'd felt moments before vanished. His *little* house? Alone? Working with him was one thing. Just sitting around tempting her raging hormones to do something stupid was an entirely different matter.

"I'm . . . I'm not really hungry. You go ahead if you want."

Truth be known, she was starving. As soon as he left, she planned to haul out the milk, fruit, crackers and peanut butter she'd picked up at the store on her way to work that morning and chow down.

He stood and then looked down at her. "I know you didn't eat any lunch. So I'm not buying that you're not hungry." He grabbed her hand and hauled her to her feet.

His unexpected move caused her to lose her balance and careen into his chest. To keep from falling, she latched onto his shoulders, just as his hands encircled her waist to steady her. Her T-shirt had slid up, and his warm palms lay against her bare midriff.

They stared into each other's eyes. The warmth of him seeped through her sweat pants as if they weren't even there. As if they stood there skin to skin. She could feel every inch of his long, muscular body pressing against her. It didn't take a college professor to conclude that their nearness had a very pronounced effect on him, too.

Rose kept telling herself to pull away, that this could give birth to nothing but problems, that things could happen that she'd regret, but her body paid no heed. Instead, she found herself enjoying the security his nearness provoked and wanting to snuggle deeper into the haven of his embrace.

Hunter stared at the woman in his arms. Her hair had come loose from the clip she'd used to confine it, and a few strands stuck to the sweat on her reddened cheeks. He brushed it away with the tip of his finger. Her lips opened just slightly, giving him just a glimpse of the straight row of white teeth behind them. When her pink tongue came out and swept across her mouth, he thought it would be his undoing. He felt himself lean toward her, wanting to touch her lips with his more than he'd ever wanted anything in his life.

"Doc? Doc Mackenzie?"

The strident call came from the foot of the stairs. They sprang apart as if someone had thrown a bucket of cold water on them.

"Hey, Doc. You up there?"

Hunter moved to the railing surrounding the top of the stairs, trying not to watch as Rose dragged her T-shirt back into place. He glanced back at her to make sure she'd finished before he answered.

"Yes, I'm up here." He leaned over the railing and peered down into the half-lit entry. "Who is it?"

"Jim Delaney. Want me to come up there?"

Hunter glanced to where Rose frantically sorted through a pile of old magazines with a concentration that was far too focused to be authentic.

"No, I'll come down." Hunter rounded the end of the railing and descended the stairs.

At the bottom, Jim stood to the side, his flashlight beam lighting the last few stairs. Just beyond the building, Hunter could see the front bumper of Jim's pickup truck, the extinguished headlight lamps peering at him like two alien's eyes.

"What's up, Jim?"

"You best take a look at this," the older man said, leading the way to the bed of the truck. He glanced at Hunter and shook his head. "You ain't gonna like this, Doc." He lowered the tailgate.

A large, gray, furry animal lay sprawled on a blanket. Spatters of blood stained the animal's coat in several places on its hind-quarters.

Hunter boosted himself into the truck. "Bring that flashlight up here."

Jim followed him into the truck's bed and then aimed the flashlight at the animal's head. It was a gray wolf.

"What happened?" Hunter's tone reflected the angry disgust he always felt when a helpless animal became a senseless target for fear.

Jim shrugged. "I found her on the side of the river road. She had two pups with her. Both dead as a doornail." Jim shifted the beam so Hunter could see more clearly. "Near as I could tell, both pups were shot, and I'm figuring she was, too."

Using the beam from the flashlight Hunter inspected her ears. "I was wondering if she was part of the gray wolf recovery program going on just north of here, but she's not tagged. The pups probably wandered off from the pack, and she went looking for them and found more than she bargained for." Hunter rolled the unconscious wolf on her other side and inspected the wound. "She's been shot in the thigh."

Hunter leaned closer to examine the wound. He ran his hands over and under her leg. "It doesn't look like the bullet damaged the bone, but there's no exit wound. The bleeding's stopped, but we need to get the bullet out to prevent infection." He jumped out of the truck, and then pulled the blanket toward him, slowly sliding the wolf's heavy body to where they could get a grip on the blanket. "Help me carry her into the office."

Jim jumped down beside Hunter, turned off his flashlight, tucked it in his jacket pocket, and then grabbed the opposite ends of the blanket. He and Hunter moved in unison and heaved the animal out of the truck. As they moved toward the office, Hunter turned his head back toward the garage.

"Rose, we have an injured animal down here. I need your help."

Upstairs, Rose had been sorting magazines trying to quell the aftermath of their close encounter, when Hunter's raised voice reached her. Hearing the urgency in his tone, she dropped the magazines she'd been transferring to the trash pile and ran down the stairs. In the illumination from the security lights, she could see the two men struggling with a large object while making their way toward the office. Quickly, she hurried after them.

Beating them to the office, she opened the door and waited while they passed through with their burden. As they did, she saw the animal and the large bleeding wound in its upper thigh. Her stomach lurched.

This was no time for her queasy stomach to act up. She swallowed down the bile rising in her throat and hurried after them to the back of the building. Having familiarized herself with the location of everything in the operating room earlier in the day, she began to immediately assemble the instruments Hunter would need to operate on the animal.

Pausing for a moment, she looked over her shoulder. "What is it?" They'd transferred the animal to the operating table, but the men blocked her view.

Hunter moved aside so she could see and then gently patted the wolf's neck. "Her Latin name is *Canis Lupus,* gray wolf. They usually travel in packs. She must have gotten separated from hers."

Now able to see the entire animal, Rose ran her hand over the blood-damp coat. The coarse fur surprised her. It had looked so soft. "Poor thing."

Jim edged toward the door. "If you've got everything under control, Doc, I'm gonna get home to the missus. She expected me for dinner an hour ago, and she'll be fit to be tied by the time I get there."

"Thanks, Jim. Would you give Fish and Wildlife a call? They'll want to know where you found her so they can pick up the pups." Hunter smiled. "And tell Sarah not to be too rough on you. You saved one of an endangered species tonight."

"I'll call F&W, and I'll tell Sarah what you said, but I don't think it's gonna make a hill of difference. She's gonna be mad as a hornet no matter what excuse I give her." Jim laughed, and then looked at Rose. "Evenin', ma'am."

"Good night." Rose watched him go.

Hunter waved to Jim, and then moved toward the sink at the side of the room. "Let me get out of this dirty shirt, and we'll get started."

"So this is how you get animals for the sanctuary."

He didn't answer, so she turned toward him. When she saw Hunter stripped to the

54

waist, a wave of heat rushed over her. She seemed to lack the will power to drag her eyes away from the glistening drops of moisture dotting his tanned skin, and the way the muscles in his arms and back rippled as he dried himself. Willing her frozen body to react, she quickly averted her gaze, but the picture of a half-clothed Hunter stayed indelibly imprinted on her mind.

Hunter slipped into a white lab coat and came to stand beside her. "I don't always get animals this way, but it's how I started the sanctuary. One day, someone brought me a raccoon to fix up, then the next thing I knew, I was overrun with wild animals needing medical care. I built the sanctuary, and they've been bringing them to me ever since."

"What happens to them after they're healthy?" She handed him a syringe filled with an anesthetic that would ensure the wolf slept through the procedure.

"I prefer that they get returned to where Mother Nature intended them to grow old and die of natural causes, but that's not always possible." He gave the wolf the injection and then passed the empty syringe back to her. "Sometimes, because they're too old or, as in Boomer's case, too young to defend and feed themselves, they're placed where I'm assured they'll be well cared for."

His tone of voice, the almost reverence with which he spoke of the sanctuary and the animals he treated, told Rose exactly what it meant to him — his life.

He slipped a soft muzzle over the wolf's jaw and secured it with a Velcro closing at the back of her head.

The muzzle disturbed Rose. "Is that really necessary?"

"I'm afraid so." He tested the Velcro by pulling on the side to make sure it remained secure. "She can exert fifteen hundred pounds of pressure per square inch with her jaw. If she came out of the anesthetic before we expect her to, she could remove one of our arms with one bite. You want to take that chance?"

Rose shook her head and looked at the muzzle doubtfully. "Will that hold her?"

"Yes, it's been tested. I wouldn't use it otherwise. Besides, the power in her jaw is when she closes it, not when she's opening it."

She sure had a lot to learn about animals, and oddly, she found herself looking forward to it. As she shaved the area around the wound, Rose made a mental note to borrow some of Hunter's books and read up on wolves and lions.

While propping the wolf's leg up so Hunter had easy access to the wound, Rose noted the enlarged mammary glands. "Does she have babies?"

"She had a couple. Jim said they were dead. Whoever shot her had better aim when it came to the pups. They probably thought she was dead, too." He stared down at the wound in the wolf's thigh. "Someday people will realize that these animals are not dangerous."

Sadness overcame Rose. She'd never considered something happening to Beth's babies, either before or after birth. To think that this mother had lost her babies was almost more than Rose could bear. Tears threatened to blur her vision. She blinked them away. What would Hunter think about her crying over an injured wolf who'd lost her puppies?

"Let's get started," Hunter said.

Hunter began the long process of removing the bullet from the wolf and repairing her flesh. From Rose's short stint as an assistant in a small clinic the first summer after she'd earned her LPN, she'd learned that doctors don't take kindly to chatter while doing surgery, so she stopped asking questions, did her job and observed.

■ ■ ■ ■

A long time later, Hunter tied off the last stitch. "She should be as good as new in a few weeks. I don't think the bullet damaged her muscles."

Rose began bandaging the wolf's thigh. "Then what?"

"We'll keep her here until she's fully recovered. Then I'll have her transported back up north to the recovery area. They'll release her so she can find her pack." He walked to the sink, stripped off the rubber gloves, dropped them in the waste basket and then washed his hands.

"You did good tonight," he told Rose.

And she had. If he hadn't been impressed before with his new assistant, her performance tonight had made that very clear. She'd stopped talking as soon as he'd picked up the scalpel, and he'd never had to tell her something more than once. But the compassion she'd shown for the wolf had probably impressed him most. Her questions, her gentle caress and the tears she'd done her best to hide, told him she truly cared about the animal.

Now, if he could just keep his hands off her, they'd have a terrific working relationship. Rose picked that precise moment to stretch her shoulders back to remove the kinks. Her breasts pushed against her T-shirt. Hunter swallowed hard and turned away.

"Are you hungry?" He removed his lab coat and quickly slipped back into his shirt.

When he turned to face her, she was staring at him openmouthed. She didn't say anything, but she didn't have to. Desire was written as clearly in her eyes as if the words had been printed across her forehead.

He cleared his throat, and she seemed to rouse from her sensual stupor.

"I'm sorry. What did you say?" She cringed at the telltale breathlessness in her voice. Why couldn't the man stay dressed when she was around?

"I asked if you're hungry?"

Once more, the image of him shirtless and sexy as all get out assaulted her. Yes, she was hungry, but she was also certain that he didn't mean the same kind of hunger she felt coursing through her.

Suddenly, a meal of peanut butter and crackers outside with one of the wild animals sounded much safer than surf and turf with Hunter in his little house.

Chapter 3

Since Hunter wouldn't take *no* for an answer, Rose accepted his invitation to join him for something to eat, but only if they ate on his front porch. She used the excuse of needing fresh air after being cooped up in the operating room for the last few hours and needing to clear the smell of the anesthetic from her nose. In actuality, she believed she'd be safer fighting her libido in the openness of the porch rather than inside the four walls of his little cottage-like house.

Too late, she discovered that the inky night, illuminated by a full moon, made the porch more intimate than a candlelit dinner. Oddly enough, despite her misgivings, she found herself relaxing, her jagged nerves soothed by the beauty of the balmy summer night, the chirping of the crickets and the monotonous creaking of the rocking chairs on the bare wood floor.

Rose washed the last bite of ham sandwich

down with a sip of icy cold sweet tea. "Hmm, that was as good as any steak dinner. Thanks." After finishing off three sandwiches to her one, Hunter set his empty plate aside. "My pleasure. But you certainly worked hard enough your first day to deserve something better than ham and cheese on rye."

Leaning back, she gazed up at the velvet sky filled with innumerable dots of winking lights. She listened to the night sounds and inhaled the fresh air. "I enjoyed the work much more than I thought I would." Realizing how heartless that must have sounded, she bolted upright and turned to face him. "Not that I took any pleasure in the wolf getting shot, mind you."

When he smiled in understanding, she leaned back, started the rocker in motion with a push of her foot and then continued her contemplation of the night sky.

"Everything about the last two days has been wonderful — learning about the animals, watching Davy with the lion cub, being able to help you save the wolf." She sighed contentedly. "I think I'm going to love living and working in Carson."

The grind of his rocker against the porch floor joined hers. "How did you find Carson anyway? It's a tiny town buried in the middle of nowhere. I'm not even sure it's on most maps."

Rose remained silent for a moment, recalling how, when Beth talked about the town where she and her mother had lived, a glow had enveloped her foster sister's face. "A girl I met in a foster home told me about it." As she spoke, she rested her hand on her stomach, her fingers moved slightly, caressing Beth's babies. She smiled. Rose would always think of them as *Beth's babies,* even though her friend's egg didn't help produce them. "We were only twelve at the time, and we used to whisper at night after lights-out. She told me about the wildflowers that grew in the meadows every spring out by the Watkins' farm, and the way the trees looked after it snowed and how Bessie Wright ran her car into a snow bank every winter and had to be towed out."

To his credit, Hunter remained silent and let her talk. That she was doing so this freely surprised her. She'd never before shared her and Beth's private moments with anyone.

"I'm sorry. I must be boring you with all this girlish reminiscing."

He reached out and grabbed her hand, enclosing it in his warm grip. "Not at all. I've lived here all my life and right now, thanks in part to Mayor Collins, my perception of the town is a bit tarnished. It's nice to see it through the eyes of someone new." He squeezed gently. "Please, go on."

Rose glanced down at their entwined hands on the arm of her rocker. For a split second, she thought about pulling away, but realized that for the first time in a long time, she felt as if she mattered to someone, but more than that, she felt safe and cared for. Enjoying the emotions too precious to relinquish so soon, she left her hand encased in his.

"Beth —"

"Beth?"

"Beth Lawrence. Did you know the Lawrences?"

Hunter shook his head. "I don't think so. I'm sorry I interrupted. Please go on."

"Beth and her mom lived in a little white house." She turned to him. "Maybe you know it. The Johnson house just south of town. A white house with green shutters, a white picket fence and yellow roses all over the yard. Her mom loved yellow roses. Beth's tire swing hung from the big maple in the back." Rose smiled at the memory of how her friend had talked about her home for hours, making it sound more like a castle than a house. "She really loved that house. Leaving it must have been one of the hardest things she'd ever done." She turned to him. "You must know of it."

Hunter's rocker stopped suddenly. He remained silent for a while and she got the distinct impression he was choosing his words before replying. Then he shook his head. "No, the house doesn't come to mind, but then tire swings and little white houses were definitely not my priorities."

Rose couldn't repress a chuckle. "Girls, right?" She had a flashing vision of Hunter, hormones raging, ogling every girl that passed and handsome as he was, no doubt being ogled in return.

"Oh, yeah. Girls, girls and more girls." The rocker started up again.

Silence blanketed them. Contented, Rose listened to an owl hooting in the dense woods bordering the sanctuary's chain-link fence. A car passed around the curve in the road at the end of the lane leading to the clinic. Its lights swept across the yard. A light breeze ruffled Rose's hair.

Hunter's soft voice broke the thoughtful silence. "What about you?"

"Me?"

"Yeah, you and boys. Don't tell me they weren't chasing you down for dates."

"I'm afraid not. School kept me too busy for dates. I guess most everyone saw me as

a bit of a bookworm. I've always loved reading and learning new things."

"Books never held any particular excitement for me back then. I was more of a
hands-on guy. Then I had to . . . Well, other
things took precedence." He laughed and
looked just the slightest bit embarrassed at
the admission.

Rose wondered what he'd been about to
say, but only for a moment. Hunter's deep-
throated laugh only deepened the contentment embracing Rose. A congenial silence
lay between them for a time before he spoke
again. "So, are you married?"

"No."

"Engaged?"

"No."

"Seeing someone?"

"No." She let go of his hand, sat up
straight and then peered at him through the
dim light. One part of her rebelled at his
inquiries. Another part reveled in the fact
that his curiosity revealed a certain degree
of interest. "Didn't you read my job application? And what does this have to do with
anything?"

He laughed again, recaptured her hand in
his, and then leaned back. "No, I didn't read
it, at least not all of it, and it doesn't have a

single thing to do with anything. I'm just nosy."

Warmth spread over her like thick honey. That laugh of his could charm fish from a pond and make them grateful they'd swallowed the hook.

You are a dangerous man, Hunter Mackenzie.

Hunter didn't have a clue as to why he'd asked her all those questions about her personal relationships. Nor did he want to explore it to find out why. Maybe he just didn't want to talk about what the Johnson house really looked like, had always looked like: the trash and weeds in the yard, the ramshackle porch — the men who came and went at all hours.

Odd that his recollection differed so much from Beth's description. Could she have just painted a picture for Rose that fit into what Beth had wanted to see? Had Beth really loved Carson all that much or had she invented the spruced-up version for Rose's sake?

"So what happened to Beth? If she liked Carson so much, why didn't she come back here with you?" He felt her stiffen, then she slowly extracted her hand from his.

When he turned to look at her, she'd leaned her head forward, her face effectively hidden behind a veil of hair. If he hadn't learned anything else about Rose in the past two days, he'd learned that she hid behind that mass of hair whenever a subject arose that she wanted to avoid.

"Rose? Did I say something —"

"No." She raised her head and favored him with a watery smile. "It's just that . . . Beth and her husband were killed in a car accident —" Her voice choked off. "I'm sorry. It still feels very new."

A sob broke from her and large tears welled in her eyes, and then cascaded down her cheeks. Her shoulders shook as she wept quietly.

If someone had reached into his chest and ripped his heart out, Hunter could not have hurt more for Rose. Hating himself for raising the subject at all, he left his rocker and went to her. He drew her up and into his arms in one gentle movement. Pressing her cheek against his chest, he held her tight, willing her sorrow into himself.

The sobs continued for some time, before they became intermittent sniffles and gasps for air. Releasing her only long enough to grab a paper napkin left over from their supper, he handed it to her, and then pulled her back into his embrace.

He hated himself for loving the way she

felt in his arms, how perfectly they seemed to fit together. He should be concentrating on her, not his testosterone-motivated reactions. But it was hard not to want to stay this way indefinitely.

"I could cut my tongue out for reminding you," he murmured into her hair.

She shook her head, then raised her tear-streaked face to his. "It's not your fault. That's the first time I've allowed myself to cry since the funeral. I guess I needed to get it out."

She neglected to add that she didn't feel an emotional outburst would be good for the babies. Her thoughts almost made her laugh. The medical background she'd acquired gave her all the information she needed to take care of Beth's babies' health. But all her education didn't tell her how to be their mother, how to love them and nurture them and always be there when they needed her.

Finding Hunter's arms far too comforting for her peace of mind, she pulled away, separating herself from him. "I'm okay now. Thanks for the shoulder."

"Anytime." He smiled that mesmerizing smile of his.

She felt an instant need to rush back into is arms, but managed to keep it under control. "Well, it's late, and I'm tired. Guess I'll say goodnight now." She stepped to the edge of the porch. "Thanks again for supper."

"Your treat next time," he said, that tantalizing grin creasing his mouth. "You sure you'll be all right?"

All right?

No. Not all right. With Hunter in her life, she wasn't sure she would ever be all right again.

Looking back at him, the moonlight illuminating his face and the breeze ruffling his hair, she wondered how she'd survive without one day giving in to the urge to see if Hunter Mackenzie's lips tasted as good as they looked.

Hunter put away the syringe he'd used to give Molly Goodwin's gray tabby cat, Thomas, an antibiotic shot for his infected eyes. Little Molly had wanted to take her pet home, but Hunter had decided to keep the animal overnight to make sure the infection hadn't spread. Using a cotton ball, he cleaned the corners of the cat's eyes with antiseptic, then replaced him in his cage and closed and latched the door.

"You need to stay out of the tall weeds," Hunter told the cat.

Thomas tilted his head, gave Hunter a haughty glance, then curled himself into a tight ball and closed his eyes.

Hunter leaned against the cage and stared down at the cat. "You're lucky. All you do is eat and sleep. No responsibilities beyond looking after yourself, no unreasonable, uncontrollable thoughts racing through your head." He straightened and sighed.

Three days had passed since the almost-kiss in the apartment and then the late night supper on Hunter's porch. Neither he nor Rose had spoken about it, and he happily left it that way. Mainly because he had no acceptable explanation for the longing that had nagged him for hours after she'd gone up to her apartment, or why he had to dog-gedly restrain himself from following her.

Rose wasn't the first woman he'd ever held and talked through some rough moments. However, she was the first woman who had made him want to go on holding her forever and to kiss her until she forgot what had stolen her smile from him. Truth be told, he hadn't had a good night's sleep since she'd walked into his office, looked him in the eye and nearly thrown up on his desk.

"Meow!"

Thomas' plaintive yowl pulled Hunter

from his thoughts and reminded him he still had patients waiting to be seen. With a sigh, he shoved Rose to the back of his mind where she would hopefully stay — until something unexpected reminded him again of his dilemma.

That afternoon, Rose watched Hunter's truck disappear down the road on his way to make a house call about a sick horse. She heaved a sigh of relief. At least for the time being he'd be gone, and she could step off the eggshells she'd been walking on since the night on the porch.

No matter how many times she told herself she had to get this attraction to Hunter under control, her traitorous body didn't seem to hear. Hunter walked into a room, and her heart sped up. Hunter smiled, and her breath caught in her chest. Hunter walked out of the room, and she felt as if the air had been sucked out behind him.

It had passed the point of ridiculous and was quickly approaching dangerous. She had to get herself back on track. Her hand went to her stomach. She had Beth's babies to think about.

"Meooow!"

Startled from her musings, Rose looked down at her feet to find Pansy winding around her legs. "What's your problem?" she asked the cat, scooping her up into her arms.

"Meooow!"

"Okay, calm down. Dinner will be served in a minute." She carried her to the back room where the animals confined in cages stayed for a few days to recover or just be watched closely for health reasons.

"Meooow!"

This time Thomas' voice rang out, quickly followed by another plaintive caterwaul from Pansy. The cat jumped from Rose's arms and raced to the cage holding Molly Goodwin's pet. The orange, tiger-striped cat wailed again as she rubbed herself across the wire cage. Thomas answered her with an ear-splitting cry.

Rose stared at them for a time. What on earth could be wrong with them? Two more wails filled the air before Rose figured it out. They were lonely. What harm would it do to let them play together for a while? "So you both want a little company, huh? Well, that's easy enough to fix."

She walked to Thomas' cage and lifted the latch, then jumped back to avoid Pansy as she sprang from the floor and landed inside the cage. The two cats rubbed against each other and the wailing ceased.

"Thank goodness," she said, her ears still ringing with the high-pitched meows. "If you don't squeal on me, I'll let you guys visit for a while, but Pansy has to leave before Hunter comes back." She closed the cage door, then walked back into the outer office to enjoy the peace and quiet and finish some paperwork she'd started in order to avoid Hunter.

She'd just begun when Davy arrived. "Hi, Miss Rose."

"Hey, Davy."

"I see Doc's truck is gone. Did he tell you what I'm supposed to do today?"

"He sure did." She pulled a pad from the pile of papers she'd been working on. "He wants you to water and feed the peacocks and the raccoons, but stay away from the wolf."

"Sadie?"

She stared at the boy. "Sadie?"

Davy grinned, his glowing cheeks throwing his freckles into prominence. "That's what I named her."

Rose fought to suppress a smile. Since Davy had been working here, he'd managed to name almost all the animals. "Okay, Sadie. Doc doesn't want you anywhere near her."

"Aw, Sadie won't hurt me. We're friends."

Rose wagged her pencil at him. "Davy, I will not take responsibility for you getting hurt on my watch. Promise me you'll keep your distance from the wolf."

He nodded reluctantly. "Okay."

"When you're through there, Doc wants you to fill in the hole the Adamsons' yellow Lab dug under the fence again."

Davy nodded and dashed out the door.

Almost immediately, the phone rang. Rose hurried to pick it up. "Good afternoon. Paws and Claws Animal Clinic. How may I help you?"

Josephine Hawks needed to update Jake's vaccinations. Rose went through several dates and times before Mrs. Hawks settled on one for the old dog's visit. During the entire conversation, Rose found her gaze drifting to the doorway through which Davy had raced moments earlier. A feeling of unease slowly formed in the pit of her stomach.

Probably just her wild imagination. However, for her own peace of mind and not because she didn't trust Davy, she decided to check on him. Rose quickly jotted Jake's name in Hunter's appointment book, then ended the conversation.

Before the phone could ring again, she clicked on the answering machine, and then followed the path Davy would have taken to the wild animal ward — a separate building set off to the side of the office to hold the animals not well enough to be put into one of the outdoor pens. Right now, only Sadie resided there.

As she stepped through the door, her breath caught in terror at the sight that met her gaze. Davy had not only begun feeding Sadie, he had chosen to do it from inside the cage with the wolf's head in his lap.

Rose froze. Hunter's description of the power in the wolf's jaw raced through Rose's mind. Her terror grew. She tried to call out to him, but stark fear had stolen her voice. She stared at the two of them in panicky silence. Her hands shook and her palms began to sweat, as she strained to speak.

"Davy." The word emerged from her tight throat as barely a squeak. She cleared her throat quietly and tried again. "Davy."

The boy looked up and grinned. "See? I told you she likes me." As if understanding Davy's words, the wolf turned her head and licked Davy's cheek from jawbone to hairline.

Rose gasped. "Get out of the cage. Do it slowly." Rose put a hand to her chest where her rapidly beating heart threatened to break free. "Don't frighten her."

"She's not afraid, Miss Rose. Watch the trick I taught her." He put a piece of meat between his teeth, then leaned toward the wolf's powerful mouth.

Fearing she'd scare the wolf and the animal would bite off Davy's face, Rose stifled the scream building in her throat.

Instead of biting the boy, the wolf rolled back her lips and gingerly took the food with her teeth. Rose's sigh of relief could be heard for miles. "Davy, please get out of Sadie's cage, now."

"It's okay, Miss Rose. Really. I've been visiting her every day, and we're friends now. Isn't that right, Sadie?" After the wolf finished chewing, she swallowed, then licked him, this time from chin to forehead. Davy laughed and wiped at his wet face with the sleeve of his cotton shirt.

Rather than calming her fears, Davy's words brought new horrors. He'd been alone in here with this wild animal, and no one had known about it. Horrific scenarios raced across her mind's eye. What if the wolf hadn't accepted him? What if she'd hurt him?

"Come on, Miss Rose." Davy motioned for Rose to come closer. "Pet her. She won't hurt you. Honest."

Rose stared at them for a long time. The boy seemed so trusting of the big animal and she of him. Could he be right? Against her better judgment, Rose took one tentative step closer to the cage. If nothing else, she'd be close enough to snatch Davy out, should it come to that.

The wolf, sensing Rose's movements, raised her head from Davy's lap, stared at her for a split second, moved her gaze to Davy, then nestled back into the comfort of her human pillow.

With that one simple gesture from the animal, Rose breathed easier. As crazy as it sounded, she'd seen the same trust and love in the wolf's eyes as she had in the eyes of their canine patients when they gazed at their owners. Unable to take her gaze from the wild creature and the little boy, she watched for a long time, still ill at ease, but trying to see this from the point of view of someone more used to interacting with animals.

The sound of a car pulling into the gravel parking lot drew her attention.

Hunter had returned.

Quelling the sudden double time of her heart and loath to leave Davy alone for one second with the wolf, she stepped into the open doorway and motioned for Hunter to join her. When he got close enough, she took his hand and pulled him into the building.

"What's going on?" Hunter asked.

She shook her head, laid a finger over her lips, then pointed at the scenario inside the wolf's cage.

Hunter's first impulse . . . Get Davy out of there. Rose stopped him with a tug on his sleeve and an empathic shake of her head. He strained against her hold, trying to step around her, but she blocked his progress.

"He's been coming here every day since the wolf came. They've made friends. He's even taught her tricks," Rose explained.

At that moment, Davy threw his little arms around the wolf and hugged her close. The wolf nuzzled his neck, then licked his ear. Her tail thumped against the straw in the bottom of the cage. Davy giggled.

Hunter relaxed. Having studied the gray wolf, he knew that the wagging tail signaled a lack of aggression. For the moment, Davy was in no danger. Still, his whole body stayed on alert to spring. Then the wolf licked Davy's face again. Hunter's jaw opened in amazement. "Well, doesn't that beat all? I guess the boy really is a Dr. Dolittle." Hunter stood behind Rose and, grasping her shoulders, looked over her head at Davy. She leaned back against him, as if the peaceful scene between animal and child had somehow seeped into her. "I've read about this happening, but it's usually with another animal or another wolf." Rose turned her head toward Hunter, an expression of confusion on her face. "She's adopted Davy as a replacement for her dead pups."

"But he's only been around her for a few days. How did he win her trust so quickly?" Rose whispered so only he could hear.

"Who knows? Some people just have a way with animals. I guess Davy's mom was right. He can charm anything with fur on it."

Rose nodded. "Too bad the townspeople can't —" Suddenly, she spun to face him, her eyes glowing with excitement. "Hunter, that's the answer."

He grinned devilishly. "I'm sorry. I seemed to have missed the question?"

She frowned. "I'm serious. This could be the way to show the people of Carson that these animals don't pose a threat to them."

He shook his head. "I'm afraid you lost me."

"They need to see this." She pointed over her shoulder toward the boy and the wolf.

"We need to show it to them. How can they argue that these animals will hurt them when a ten-year-old boy can safely sit in the same cage with an eighty-pound wild wolf?"

Mesmerized by the sparkle in her eyes and the excited expression on her face, Hunter leaned against the doorway, keeping Davy and the wolf in his line of vision, and crossed his arms over his chest. "And exactly how would you suggest we do that?"

"I don't know. You're the vet. Think of something."

He *was* thinking of something, but it had nothing to do with the people of Carson or Davy or Sadie. It did, however, have everything to do with Rose Hamilton, and how tempting her lips were, and how much he wanted to hold her again and find out for himself if making love to her would be even close to the exquisite experience it had been in his dreams.

Then what she said began to penetrate the sensual haze surrounding his brain. Anger rose up in him, an old anger that had been brought to the surface in the last few days by his conversations with George Collins. "These people don't want to be educated. They want to keep things exactly as they've always been while they sit in their safe little houses and worry about no one

80

but themselves. What they do want is to get rid of the sanctuary."

She stared at him in shock. "So your solution is to just sit back and let them force you to shut down? Is that it?"

"I'm not just sitting back."

"What are you doing, besides dodging George Collins' phone calls and, when you can't do that, trading angry words with him that only makes the problem worse?"

Before he could retort, a car pulled into the parking lot. Sheriff Ben Ainsley stepped from the black and white car. He glanced at them, then came slowly toward them. Rose and Hunter met him half way.

"Ma'am. Hunter." He tapped the brim of his Mountie-style gray hat.

"Ben, what brings you out this way?" Hunter had a sinking sensation that the visit had something to do with the animals and George Collins.

"I'm sorry, Doc, but the mayor sent me out here to collect his boy."

Rose stepped to Hunter's side, her face defiant. "Why?"

"Let me handle this," Hunter said, taking her arm.

"Ma'am —"

She pulled free of Hunter's grasp and took another step toward the sheriff. "I'm Rose

Hamilton, Dr. Mackenzie's assistant." Rose raised her chin mutinously and faced off with the man towering above her, looking every bit like a wild animal about to do battle for her babies. "Why do you want Davy?"

"Ms. Hamilton." The chief tapped his hat brim once more. "The *why* of it doesn't matter. The fact is that Davy's ten, and the mayor's his daddy and my boss. His daddy wants him out of here, and he sent me to see to it." He looked around the grounds. "Where's the boy, Doc?"

Rose opened her mouth to say more, but Hunter stopped her with a shake of his head. No sense fighting it. He'd been expecting something like this ever since Davy had come to work for him.

"He's in there." Hunter motioned over his shoulder in the direction of the building behind them.

Just then, a fierce growl emanated from inside, followed by Davy's high-pitched scream.

CHAPTER 4

Rose beat both Sheriff Ainsley and Hunter to the door of the building where Davy and the wolf were. She rushed through the door and stopped dead, her breath trapped in her throat.

"Oh, my God!"

Seated in a corner, Davy had plastered his body against the side of the cage, his arms crossed over his chest in a defensive posture. His face had taken on an ashen cast, his eyes large and terrified. Sadie stood over him. Saliva dripped from her mouth. Her low, threatening growl seemed to echo off the cement block walls.

"Lord have mercy," Sheriff Ainsley muttered.

"Stay here." Hunter eased past Rose and the sheriff and started toward the cabinet at the side of the room.

Rose grabbed his arm. "You'll frighten her."

"Not if I move slowly. I need to get to the tranquilizer gun I keep in the drawer over there." He pointed to a cabinet almost even with where the wolf held Davy captive.

Hunter pulled his arm from Rose's grasp. She watched in terror as, never taking his gaze off the occupants of the cage, he inched toward the cabinet.

Rose held her breath. She could hear her heart thumping wildly in her ears. Everything seemed to move in slow motion, including Hunter's progress toward the cabinet. As he neared the cabinet, the wolf shifted her body, blocking Rose's view of the little boy.

"Don't move, Davy," Hunter told the boy, his voice low and calm.

"It's okay, Doc." Davy's voice, though weak and subdued, held no fear. "Sadie was protecting me."

Hunter stopped. "Protecting you from what?"

"Show him, girl. Show the doc what you caught."

Obediently Sadie swung her big head toward Hunter. A three-foot snake dangled from the wolf's mouth.

"Well, I'll be. Sadie killed a snake."

Rose couldn't believe her ears, but then the wolf walked to the side of the cage and with a jerk of her head, threw the dead snake out of the open cage door. It landed at Hunter's feet. Gingerly, he picked up the lifeless reptile. Sadie turned away, lay down beside Davy and rested her head in his lap.

Holding it up so Rose and the sheriff could see it, Hunter announced, "It's a copperhead."

Rose fought off the chill creeping down her back. Not wanting to get close to it even though it was obviously dead, she kept her distance. "Is it dangerous?"

"Not anymore, but alive it's very dangerous," Hunter said, carrying the reptile to her. "Although they are not usually aggressive. They're normally more interested in mice and lizards. My guess is she chased a rodent in here and came face to face with Sadie."

Still maintaining a safe distance, Rose inspected the snake. Its coppery-orange coloring and the hourglass-shaped markings on its back made it almost attractive. If any snake could be thought of in those terms.

The sheriff, who had been stunned into openmouthed awe at the sight of a huge timber wolf acting like a pet dog with Davy, shook himself free of the fear that had immobilized him. "The boy said the wolf protected him."

"She did." Davy exited Sadie's cage. Sadie followed like a faithful puppy. Rose and the sheriff took a couple of steps back. "She won't hurt you." Davy turned to the wolf and hugged her enormous neck. "Will ya, girl?" The wolf licked his face.

Sheriff Ainsley removed his hat and scratched his head. "Well, if that don't beat all."

Rose finally relaxed enough to speak. "What happened, Davy?"

He grinned at Rose like a proud parent. "I was sitting there petting Sadie, when all of a sudden she jumped up and started growling at the corner of the cage. Then I saw that snake sliding across the floor. It came straight for me, and the next thing I knew, Sadie had it in her mouth."

Hunter laughed. "Well, Sheriff, you still want to haul Davy out of here?"

Rose again held her breath. If the sheriff took Davy away, what would Sadie's reaction be to being separated from the boy?

Davy looked from one to the other. "Haul me off where?"

"Never mind, Davy. I don't think you could be anywhere safer than right here." The sheriff tipped his hat. "I'll be seeing you folks."

"But what about —" Rose started.

"What he doesn't know won't hurt him. I'll tell him I couldn't find the boy." The sheriff winked at Davy and then left.

Rose leaned against the wall, too drained emotionally by the events of the past half hour to stand on her own. "Well, I don't know about you two, but I've had enough excitement for today."

Davy and Hunter laughed.

Hunter put his arm around the boy. "I think you need to put Sadie back in her cage and then get on home."

Reluctantly, Davy led Sadie back to her cage, hugged her neck and then shooed her inside and latched the door. The wolf obeyed the boy as if she were a big old dog. "Night, Sadie. See ya tomorrow." The wolf threw back her head and howled plaintively. Davy looked imploringly at Hunter. "I can't go yet. I didn't finish feeding the other animals."

"Rose and I will make sure they get fed. It's late, and we don't want to worry your mom." Hunter steered the boy toward the door. "We'll see you tomorrow."

Davy threw one last glance at Sadie, said goodnight and left.

"That's some relationship he's got going with that wolf." Rose had regained her footing and managed to move away from the support of the wall.

"Yes, it is." Hunter stared at the wolf. "I've heard of wolves befriending humans, but I don't recall one quite as unique as this one before." Then he laughed. "Maybe his mother is right. Maybe he is a Dr. Littledo in more ways than just not cleaning his room. He certainly is something else with animals, that's for sure."

Silence fell between them. Without a word, they went about feeding the animals. Not until they were finished did Rose suddenly become acutely aware of being alone with the man who seemed to have a strange pull on her emotions.

She put away the feed bags, washed her hands and wiped them on a towel, then turned to Hunter. "Well, I better get home." As though *home* were miles away and not just across the courtyard.

"I'll walk with you." Hunter placed a hand in the middle of her back and guided her to the door.

The spot where his hand rested felt like someone had applied a heating pad turned on high to her skin. She walked faster to sever the contact. "Thanks, but I can find my way on my own," she said and hurried off, her breath coming and going as fast as her feet ate up the distance to her new garage apartment. "See you tomorrow," she called back over her shoulder.

"Yeah. Tomorrow." Hunter watched her until she disappeared up the flight of stairs to her apartment. He might be wrong, but it appeared as if Ms. Hamilton couldn't get away from him fast enough.

Behind him, Sadie howled plaintively, obviously still protesting the departure of the most important human in her life.

"I know just how you feel, Sadie." What Hunter didn't know was why he was allowing his emotions to get all tangled up with a woman, something he'd sworn would never happen. Emotional attachments meant relationships, and relationships grew into marriage, then family and a ton of responsibilities he didn't want.

He thought back to the time when, after his parents' accident, he'd been saddled with raising his two younger teenage siblings and what the demands on him as the oldest, the father figure, entailed. He'd had no time for himself and even had to wait until they were both in college before he could fulfill his dream of becoming a vet. Thankfully, one of them had won a scholarship, and the other had insisted on paying his own way through university, otherwise there wouldn't have been any money left over for Hunter. As it turned out, what money they had only put him through two semesters, and he had to pay for the rest with a couple of part-time jobs, one at a local fast-food joint and the other working weekends on a garbage truck.

Not that he didn't love his sister and brother, he did. And not that he wouldn't have used the money to pay for their education if it had come down to that. He would have walked over hot coals for them. He was just bone-tired of being their parent. Repairing broken household appliances, cleaning out the gutters of a house, refereeing battles between them, rushing off to the ER when one of them got hurt, and then trying to figure out where the money would come from to pay for it were definitely *not* on his must-do-to-be-happy list. He'd been there and found nothing to be happy about.

After the chaos of raising them, he found he liked his quiet life among creatures that didn't demand anything from him except food, water and an occasional pat on the head, and he wanted to keep it that way.

With this unprecedented attraction he felt for Rose, he could easily see himself getting involved with her and then slipping back into that smothering family lifestyle before he could blink. In the future, he'd stop playing with fire and keep a tighter rein on his emotions. He'd treat Rose as an employee, nothing more.

Several weeks later, Hunter realized that George Collins hadn't called in days. The patient list had been full, but not overly demanding. Rose seemed to be settling into running a vet's office with an amazing efficiency. Most of all, with his resolve to stay away from Rose except for work related times still firmly in place, things at the Paws and Claws Clinic had settled into a smooth routine.

Or so Hunter thought until he decided that a lull in appointments would give him time to do the long put off spaying of Pansy, the once-stray office cat. Though Pansy had only been around the office for the past couple of weeks, she seemed to have a sixth sense about when she was up for some medical procedure, be it her rabies shots or her flea prevention treatment, and made herself scarce.

Today proved different. Pansy, who had, until today, not been an affectionate cat, had spent the day winding in and out of Hunter's legs to the point that he'd been afraid of stepping on her. At the moment, she sat between his feet, purring like a motorboat and seemingly without a care in the world or any indication that she was about to become an *it.*

Slipping his hands around her belly, he chuckled, shook his head and then hoisted her into his arms. As he carried her toward the examination table, he scratched her tummy. "I know you're not gonna like — What the heck?" He could feel knobs in her tummy. Lumps, as if she'd swallowed a bunch of small rocks.

He didn't have to guess twice about what it could be. Pansy was pregnant, but it didn't make sense. She couldn't be pregnant. Due to the danger the wild animals presented if she should wander into their cages, she hadn't been outside the office since she first came in. She was the only cat in the place, except for some patients who'd been here. But they were always in cages.

He placed Pansy on the examination table and rolled her to her back. Carefully he inspected her nipples. Bright pink and enlarged. Then he felt for the lumps he'd detected in her tummy. They were small, but under his skilled fingers, he couldn't mistake what they were . . . the heads of several tiny kittens. He estimated a litter of about four, perhaps five.

For a moment he stared at the cat. Bad enough that this had happened to Pansy. What if it had been a customer's pet? There had better be a very good explanation for this.

Anger barely in check, he left Pansy on the examination table and hurried to the front office. Rose had her head bent over the keyboard, entering data into a patient's file.

"How did Pansy get pregnant?"

Rose jumped and jerked around to face him. "Excuse me?"

"How did Pansy get pregnant?"

The corner of Rose's mouth twitched in a half smile. "I didn't think I'd have to explain to you how that works, Dr. Mackenzie."

Her addressing him as *Dr. Mackenzie* only increased his anger. She'd taken to calling him that in the past weeks, and while he was certain it was a by-product of his businesslike attitude of late, the formality grated on his nerves. Nor did he like the fact that she seemed to be making light of Pansy's condition.

"I know how she got pregnant. What I want to know is . . . *how* she got pregnant." He sounded like an idiot.

Rose looked puzzled.

"How did it happen?" He took a deep

breath. "Who did it happen with? She never goes out and no males are in here except for treatments and then they're either receiving treatment or always in cages. So who's the daddy? Have you let her outside?"

Rose frowned and shook her head. Then suddenly her eyes got large, and she clamped her hand over her mouth. It reminded him of the first day she'd stepped into the clinic. Was she going to be sick?

Just as quickly, she removed her hand. "I think I'm to blame."

"What?"

Rose held up her hand. "No, not for her pregnancy, just for making it . . . possible."

His frustration level about at the breaking point, Hunter ran a hand through his hair and took the seat at the desk beside Rose.

Modulating his tone, he asked, "What exactly do you mean by *possible?*"

Straightening her shoulders, Rose swiveled her chair to face him squarely. She scooped a lock of hair off her face and tucked it behind her ear, then folded her hands in her lap. "Well . . . I . . . uh . . . You see, Thomas, Molly Goodwin's tabby cat . . . Well, he was meowing, and Pansy was meowing. I thought they might be lonely, so I kind of put them in the same cage to play for a while." She spit out the last few words as if the faster she said them the less trouble she'd be in.

Hunter bolted to his feet. "You what?"

"In my defense, I didn't know what their problem was, and I was just trying to shut them up so I could get some work done, and they were very quiet after I . . . put . . . them . . ." She dropped her face to her hands. "Oh, crap. I am so sorry." Then she raised her gaze to him. "Are you going to fire me?"

Her abject remorse coupled with the reminder that she'd never been around animals before and couldn't be expected to know the warning signs of a cat in heat, served to cool Hunter's anger. "No, I'm not going to fire you. Just please, talk to me before you do anything like that again."

"There is an upside." Rose smiled weakly. "Pansy will be a mom, and we'll have a cute little litter of kitties around here."

His anger began to surface again. "Maybe Pansy doesn't want to be a mom and have the responsibility of caring for babies. Maybe she just wanted to go on being a loner and having a life of her own, catching mice and —" He stomped from the office, slamming the connecting door behind him, and leaving Rose to stare wide-eyed after him.

She frowned. What on earth had brought that on? One minute he'd seemed to have been cooling off, and the next he'd erupted like an active volcano. All she'd said was that Pansy would be a mom. For some reason, that had set him off again. And what a strange choice of words. The way he'd ranted on about it, anyone would think he'd been talking about a human and not a cat.

By the end of the day Hunter had not come out of the back room, so Rose finished up her chores and had started to get ready to close the office. She'd just clicked on the answering machine, when Hunter emerged from the back. Fearing another eruption, she busied herself straightening papers and pretended not to notice him.

He cleared his throat, forcing her to acknowledge his presence. "Rose, I want to apologize for my totally irrational reaction to Pansy's pregnancy." Then he smiled, and, as if by magic, the man she'd called Hunter appeared.

"No problem. We all have our moments."

"Well, be that as it may, it wasn't fair to yell at you. I should have spayed Pansy when I took her in, but I kept putting it off. So this is just as much my fault as anyone's." He stared at her for a long moment. "Let me make it up to you by cooking you one of the thick steaks I have in the fridge."

Rose knew she should say *no.* Her equilibrium couldn't withstand being near him in a casual setting away from the office. But she wanted so desperately to say *yes.* These past few weeks of formal conversation had been the longest of her life. She longed for the relaxed atmosphere that had existed between them on that first day. But did she dare?

"I'd love to." Good grief! Where had that come from? Oh well, in for a dime, in for a dollar . . . or however that saying went. She couldn't back out gracefully now.

"Great. I'll start the grill, and that'll give you time to freshen up before dinner." He opened the front door for her.

As she stepped into the doorway, their gazes locked. His warm breath feathered across her hot cheeks. She became way too aware of the width of his chest and the deep smile grooves around his full lips.

Dragging her gaze away, she hurried through the door. "I'll make a salad," she called as she dashed toward the garage and the emotional safety of her apartment. Hopefully, she could get herself under control before she had to sit across a table from him.

CHAPTER 5

Showered and dressed in white shorts and a pale salmon T-shirt, Rose finished throwing the cut-up salad vegetables into a large wooden bowl she'd found among the kitchen utensils that Hunter had said she could use. She added dressing, and then tossed the veggies thoroughly. Firming up her resolve to keep this dinner on a friendly basis, she picked up the bowl and descended the stairs into the yard connecting the garage to the main house.

Still unsure about the prudence of spending the evening with Hunter, she covered the distance slowly. One of the main reasons she'd agreed to have dinner with him had been because she'd grown tired of her own company. Since the incident with Davy and the wolf weeks ago, Hunter had become a different person from the man who'd hired her. He'd closeted himself with patients and then closed up shop at the end of the day and disappeared inside his house. She would retire to her apartment and watch TV or read.

She hadn't expected life here to be a never-ending action adventure, but she had hoped for at least a friendship with the handsome vet. Something on a neighborly level.

Liar!

The word shot through her brain like a Fourth of July rocket.

Ever since you first saw him, he's been on your mind. Admit it! You want far more than a neighborly level *with this man.*

But that can't be. Rose ran her hand over her flat tummy. She could no longer think in *me* terms. It was now *us.* Her and the twin lives she carried inside her. How could she even consider a future with any man until she'd settled her own life? Until she discovered if she had any mommy genes in her or if she had inherited those of the mother who had walked out on her claiming she *just couldn't do this.*

Rose shook away the troubling thoughts. Hunter had done nothing to make her think he had any interest in her. Nothing besides giving her a job, a place to live and an income to support herself and eventually the babies. There had been no hint of anything beyond a very strict employer/employee relationship, and she planned to keep it that way. Still, they could be friends. Couldn't they?

As she grew closer to his house, she skirted the front and headed toward the backyard where, having seen him cooking on other evenings, she knew he kept the barbeque grill. The smell of cooking meat enveloped her. If nothing else, the vet evidently had some cooking skills. She hadn't smelled anything half as mouth-wateringly enticing in a very long time.

Stepping around the corner of the house, Rose came to a sharp halt in the shadow of a large maple tree shading the patio. Hunter stood at the grill, his hair still shower-damp, his broad shoulders encased in a lemon-yellow T-shirt, his feet bare and his tanned legs exposed by snug denim shorts. All her good intentions to keep this on a friendly basis threatened to sail right off into the twilit night.

Taking a deep breath, she stepped out of the shadows onto the patio stones. "Salad has arrived." She held up the bowl.

Hunter swung around. For a moment he stared at her as if he'd never seen her before, then gave his head a slight shake and grinned. "Great. Looks wonderful," he added after peeking into the bowl. Then he gestured toward a table he'd already set with plates, silverware, glasses and citronella candles, which infused the night air with an exotic aroma. "Put it over on the table. The steaks should be ready in just a few minutes. There's a bottle of wine cooling in the ice bucket. Why don't you pour us each a glass?"

Rose placed the salad bowl on the table, then filled one glass half way with the chilled white zinfandel, and carried it to the grill for him. He glanced at her other empty hand. "You're not having any?"

How did she tell him that she didn't want it because pregnant women don't drink alcohol? She opted for a vague refusal. "I'm not much of a drinker. Got any soda?"

He nodded, laid the tongs on the side of the grill and disappeared inside. Moments later, he emerged with a can of Coke. "Here you go."

When she took it, his fingers slid over hers, and the resulting tingle traveled all the way to her shoulder. The unexpected sensation totally unnerved her. Quickly, she retreated back to the table and sat in one of the chairs. She stared at his broad back and wondered how she'd ever get through this night without grabbing him and seeing if his kisses would be as sweet as she'd imagined.

Hunter felt Rose's gaze burning into his back. Doing his best to look casual, he flipped the steaks and concentrated on the task at hand. Not easy while still trying to recover from the unexpected sight of her luscious tanned legs and all that long, auburn hair spilling over her shoulders and onto her breasts . . .

He shook himself. *Steaks. Cook the steaks. She's just another woman.*

But that was the problem. She wasn't *just* another woman. She was Rose, the woman who'd been living in his head since the day she walked into the clinic. The woman that threatened to make him forget all his resolve about family.

Keeping away from her this past week had been torture. He'd lain in bed at night, knowing she lay in her bed only a few hundred yards away in the apartment. He worked in the back of his office all too aware of the scent of her perfume that wafted into the back room every time he opened the office door. How could he possibly keep his emotions under control with the temptation of having her close, yet not nearly close enough?

■ ■ ■ ■

The sun had gone down and a soft breeze blew up through the valley. In the distance, the silhouette of Hawks Mountain loomed against the deep purple night sky. Hunter couldn't remember when he'd felt more relaxed and content.

"You're some kind of chef, Dr. Mackenzie." She saluted him with her soda can.

He returned the salute and took a drink.

Rose traced circles in the sweat on the can, and then tilted her head. "May I ask a question?"

A bit anxious about what the question would be, he lowered the glass and nodded. "Sure."

Rose hesitated, looked down at the can, then met his gaze with her own. "Why did you get so upset about Pansy's pregnancy?"

Knowing he would eventually have to offer some rational reason why he'd acted like a jerk, he put his half-empty wine glass on the table and leaned toward her. "Rose, about that . . . I am really sorry for my attitude this afternoon. I know you haven't had much experience with animals, and you couldn't have known what would inevitably happen between Pansy and Thomas."

She nodded and smiled. "Apology accepted." Then she looked as if she wanted to say more.

He tilted his head. "But?"

"Well, it just seemed . . . I felt it was . . . a little over the top." Rose spit out the last words as if afraid she'd lose her nerve. "I mean, you seemed to take it personally."

Stalling for time, Hunter refilled his glass. Then he stood and walked to the edge of the patio, his back to Rose, his face lifted to the sparkling night sky. In retrospect, he agreed with Rose. His reaction had been over the top . . . and personal. But having a family thrust upon Pansy seemed to have brought back the painful memories of the days when he had fought for a life of his own. The days of laundry, grocery lists, homework, sports schedules, and curfews and two semi rebellious teenagers who needed a parent figure. None of which Pansy would have to contend with, but nevertheless a grim reminder of how his own life had been stolen from him by a man who'd had too many beers and not enough sense to stay out from behind the wheel of his car.

"Hunter?"

Rose's voice pulled him from his thoughts. He sighed and returned to the table.

Taking a sip of wine to stiffen his back-bone, he began his tale. "When I was twenty, both my parents were killed in a car accident with a drunk driver, leaving me to raise my sixteen-year-old sister Janice and seventeen-year-old brother Kenny . . . alone."

Rose's hand closed over his. "I'm so sorry."

As if he were afloat in unfriendly waters and her hand was a life preserver, he curled his fingers around hers. "Thanks." He took a deep breath and continued. "As the oldest, the responsibility for keeping the remains of our family together and taking on the responsibilities of both mother and father fell to me." He dropped her hand and leaned back in his chair. "Unfortunately, that meant putting my life on hold until my siblings had theirs in order and stretching what little money my parents left us to cover college expenses."

"That must have been very hard on you."

Hunter laughed derisively. "I didn't mind . . . at first. Thank God, both of them were reasonably good kids so I never ended up at the police station at four in the morning bailing them out. But it got harder and harder as the months went by. There never seemed to be enough money for everything.

Janice did what she could around the house, and Kenny got a part-time job after school."

"What about college? You obviously have a degree in veterinary medicine, but what about your sister and brother?"

"Janice won a scholarship, and Kenny worked his way through." He shrugged. "After they were on their way, I started college and financed it with part-time jobs. It wasn't easy, but we managed." He paused and stared off into the night. "What finally got to me was the responsibility of all of it."

Suddenly, it all came rushing back. The weight of the burden he'd assumed for his dead parents, the underlying, nagging knowledge that if he messed up, two lives could be ruined. He'd lain awake many nights wondering if he'd done the right thing, wondering if his decision would come back to bite him and Janice and Kenny.

"So where are Janice and Kenny now?"

He smiled. "Janice is teaching school in upstate New York, and Kenny holds a master's degree in business and owns a couple of hotels on the West Coast."

Rose again covered his hand with hers. "Sounds to me like you did a pretty good job."

He shrugged. "I suppose. But I'd never do it again. The strain of all that responsibility was a lot more than I could stand, and something I don't want to experience again." He sat up straight, shedding the troubles of a life gone by, picked up the wine bottle and then paused and asked Rose, "Another soda?"

Rose placed her hand on top of her can and shook her head. "No, I've had my limit, thanks."

She watched Hunter as he poured a small amount of zinfandel into his own glass. She was finally coming to understand Hunter Mackenzie a bit better, and what she'd found out tonight explained a lot. Hunter didn't want a family . . . ever.

An empty feeling settled inside her. She hadn't expected anything to come of their tenuous friendship, or so she'd been telling herself. Now she had to admit that there had been a tiny glimmer of hope. Otherwise, why would she feel so overwhelmingly disappointed, so utterly alone? Suddenly the star-studded heavens and the balmy night that had lulled them both into a state of contented relaxation seemed to be mocking her with promises of other nights like this, nights that could never be. She had to bite her lip to keep from crying out at the injustice of it all.

She smoothed her hand over her tummy.

107

Obviously Hunter loved his job and the animals. But the one thing Hunter didn't care for was the responsibility of a family. If there had been any hope of a relationship before, the two tiny lives inside her and her promise to their mother had effectively extinguished it.

The following day, Rose breathed a sigh of relief when it seemed that Hunter had returned to his good-humored self. He no longer closeted himself in the back, and he chatted with her amiably between patients.

Around three, the office door opened, and a woman with gray hair and a cheery smile entered with a shaggy gray dog in tow. Rose glanced at the appointment book. Josephine Hawks and her dog Jake.

"Hello, Ms. Hawks."

"Granny Jo will do nicely. It's what everyone calls me." The friendly tone of the woman's voice flowed over Rose like warm water. She knew nothing about Granny Jo, but she liked her already.

"Jake's here for his rabies booster and heartworm check." She patted the old dog lovingly on the head. He leaned his shaggy body against her leg, forcing her to clutch the edge of the desk to keep her balance. "Well, glory be, Jake. Knock me over why don't you." She made a *tsking* sound, and then centered her sharp gaze back on Rose. "And who might you be?"

Rose smiled. "I'm Rose. Rose Hamilton. Dr. Mackenzie's new assistant and receptionist."

Granny Jo nodded. "That's right. I heard Donna ran off to get married." Then she grinned wider. "Seems to be a lot of that goin' round these days. My granddaughter Becky will be tying the knot come the end of summer. Matter of fact, she just picked out her gown last week."

The pride and love in the old woman's voice and face made Rose wonder what it would have been like to have grown up with a family around her, a blood family. A family that would have loved and protected her, encouraged her in her career choice, and been there when life got too tough to handle alone. But, by the luck of the draw, she had no idea who her father was and had ended up with a mother with no mothering genes.

"Granny Jo!"

Hunter's entrance drew both women's attention.

He gave Granny a hug, then patted Jake's head. "How's his leg doing?"

"Good as new. You did a fine job patching him up. Spends most of his days out chas-

109

ing anything with four legs around the woods."

Rose handed Hunter the dog's chart. "Jake is here for his booster and a heart-worm check."

Hunter took the file and gave her a smile. Her heart jumped. She returned his smile, then quickly averted her eyes. Unfortunately, not before Granny Jo caught the exchange. The old woman raised one eyebrow, but said nothing.

"Come on, Jake." Hunter latched onto Jake's collar. "You and I will take care of business while the ladies stay out here and chat." He glanced at Rose and then led the dog through the door into the back of the office.

Granny Jo settled herself in one of the plastic chairs. After putting her purse on the floor beside her, she folded her hands in her lap and then studied Rose. A few moments passed before she finally spoke. "So, what's going on with you and the doc?"

Startled, Rose snapped her gaze to the old woman's. "Excuse me?"

"Young lady, there's two things I know for sure. The sun's going down tonight and coming up tomorrow. And when two people look at each other like you two just did, there's more going on than just a working relationship."

"Wow! You don't beat around the bush, do you?"

"No time. I'm not getting any younger. When I have something to say, I say it."

Rose tipped her head so her hair hid the side of her face from Granny Jo and pretended to be engrossed in the paperwork on her desk.

"Well?"

Heat burned in Rose's cheeks. She tossed the hair off her face with a twist of her head. "I'm afraid your intuition or radar or whatever you call it is wrong this time. There's absolutely nothing going on." *And not because I wouldn't welcome it.*

Again, one of Granny's gray eyebrows arched. "Right, and at this very moment my Jake isn't licking the doc's cheek trying to sweet talk him out of that rabies booster." But she didn't press the subject. Rose breathed a relieved sigh and went back to work.

A half hour later, Hunter emerged from the back with Jake at his heels and turned him over to Granny Jo. "He's all set. No heartworm, his leg has mended just fine and even though he tried to talk me out of the booster shot by washing my face with kisses, we got that done, too." He leaned down and scratched behind Jake's ear.

Rose stole a glance at Granny Jo, and this time both the old woman's eyebrows were raised. And she smiled like a Cheshire cat.

CHAPTER 6

The next morning passed fairly uneventfully. Outside appointments filled Hunter's day and kept him out of the office. Davy arrived after lunch and had been engulfed in feeding the animals and making his usual visit to Sadie before heading home. Since Rose didn't expect Hunter back until late afternoon, she'd spent the day rearranging the filing cabinets, which kept her mind off her handsome boss and what Granny Jo had inferred about Rose's feelings for him.

Hunter's previous receptionist had her own system, one that made it necessary for Rose to spend a lot of time looking for files in the wrong place, such as Martha Cramer's file under the *M*'s instead of the *C*'s. Or Bubba Benson's file under *L* for Lilac, his cow.

This lull had been the perfect opportunity to establish a system that made some sense. It had taken up all of her morning and most of the afternoon, but she was finally down to the last pile of manila folders. With no in-house appointments, by the time Davy finished feeding the animals, she'd be ready to call it a day, and they could close up shop and go home.

Exasperated that anyone could view this filing system as efficient, Rose picked up the last pile of folders, flopped them on her desk, sat and then began arranging them alphabetically according to the first initial of the pet owner's last name. Just then, the four overnight patients in the back room began to raise a fuss, which quickly escalated into a who-can-bark-louder-and-longer contest. Irritated by the noisy distraction and recalling how Hunter had calmed them down the first day she'd been here, Rose smacked the wall behind her. Her palm stung, but the barking ceased immediately, and she went back to work.

Only five minutes or so had passed when the front door burst open and banged against the wall. Rose jumped and looked up ready to reprimand Davy for his noisy entrance. But it wasn't Davy . . . at least not *just* Davy.

A fairly large, marginally good-looking man dressed in a three-piece, navy suit; white shirt and red power tie filled the doorway. Clutched in the man's right hand, the toes of his sneakers barely touching the floor, hung a tearful, squirming Davy.

"Let me go!"

The man glared down at the boy. "Quiet!"

"Mackenzie!" His bellow vibrated off Rose's eardrums. "Mackenzie!"

Three-piece suit. Attitude out the ying-yang. Having the audacity to be physical with Davy. Not to mention, she'd talked enough on the phone with him that she'd recognize that voice anywhere. This had to be none other than Hunter's nemesis, George Collins, the mayor of Carson.

Rose stood, glanced at Davy and then threw Collins a scathing look. "Dr. Mackenzie is out of the office today on house calls. I'm Rose Hamilton, his receptionist." It took every ounce of control inside her to keep her voice even and not scream "Child abuse!" then vault the desk and tear Davy from his grasp.

"I want to see Mackenzie . . . Now." he sneered.

"I already told you, he's out of the office for the day and before you'll get any further help from me, you'll have to let go of the boy. You're hurting him." She glared at Collins. He glared back, but she refused to back down. Instead, she pursed her lips to let him know that nothing would pass them until the boy was released.

Anger shot from his eyes like darts from a dart gun. He let go of Davy, and the boy had to grab the desk to keep from falling to his knees. "Happy?"

Davy skittered away from his father's reach to the far side of the room.

Rose nodded. "Now, what can I do for you?"

"You can tell Mackenzie I want to talk to him."

Struggling to keep her temper in check, she took a deep, cleansing breath and modified her tone. "I've already told you he's not here today. Can I give him a message?"

"You can. You can tell him that Davy quit!" Collins made no effort to harness his anger.

Determined not to show this bully any fear, Rose straightened her spine. Besides, he might be willing to look like a jerk in front of his son, but she wasn't.

Very calmly, she asked, "And the reason would be . . ."

Her question seemed to fuel his anger. He charged the desk. Though he towered at least a full foot over her, Rose stood her ground. "The reason would be that I won't have my son hanging around animals that could eat him."

"Really, Mr. Collins, they —"

"Mayor Collins."

Rose could have sworn his chest expanded a few sizes.

This bully's intimidation tactics might work on the town council, but they weren't going to work on her. She'd grown up in foster homes with some pretty tough kids and had learned how to handle guys who thought yelling and shaking a fist could get them what they wanted.

She forced a complacent smile. "Mr. Collins. Those animals are harmless babies. None of them will hurt Davy. He loves them, and they love him."

"Really? Well, I just found him in a cage with a wolf that I would hardly call a baby."

Darn! She'd forgotten about Sadie.

"It was snarling and growling like it was gonna eat me."

"Well, I can see she didn't." Obviously, even the wolf had limits.

He slammed his palm on the desk. Despite herself, Rose flinched. "This is no joking matter."

"No, it's not. If the way you dragged him in here is anything to go by, then Sadie was upset because you were probably manhandling Davy."

George's face was nearly crimson. "He's my kid, and if I want to manhandle him, I will. No wolf is gonna stop me."

Oh no? Give her half a chance, and she'll have you for lunch, you pompous . . . Rose's tightly controlled temper broke loose. "Well, she may not stop you, but I will."

George leaned closer, bringing his face mere inches from Rose's. "And exactly how do you plan to do that, Missy?"

"I suggest you back off, Collins. Now!"

Both Rose and Collins swung toward the stern voice coming from behind George. Hunter stood just inside the door, glaring at George. Evidently the rage in Hunter's expression hit home with Collins. He backed away from Rose, grabbed Davy and headed for the door.

"You haven't heard the last of this," he snarled at Hunter as he squeezed past him and stalked to his car with Davy in tow.

"I'm sure I haven't," Hunter murmured.

Rose went to stand beside him. Both of them watched as George started his car and peeled out of the parking lot, leaving a plume of dust behind.

When George's silver Lexus had disappeared through the gate, she turned to Hunter. "What do you think he'll do?"

Hunter shrugged. "I don't know, but,

knowing him as I do, I can tell you for sure that it won't be pleasant."

Starting with the day after Collins' visit, a ball of dread formed in Rose's stomach every time the phone rang. Both she and Hunter had been on edge waiting for George Collins' other custom-made wingtip to drop. But to their surprise and relief, as the day passed, nothing happened. However, a gut feeling told Rose that George's parting threat had been a valid one, and they had not heard the last of him.

Late in that afternoon, a car pulling up outside drew Rose's attention. She recognized the driver immediately as Lydia Collins, Davy's mom. She'd brought Davy to work several times when the weather had been bad, and he couldn't ride his bike.

Lydia had become something of a local celebrity since she'd started doing a show for the talk radio station in Charleston. Rose listened to the show faithfully and felt as though she already knew Lydia.

"Hi!" Lydia smiled as she came through the door followed by Davy.

"Hi! What brings you here?"

"Davy's come to ask if he can have his job back." Lydia smiled down at her son, her expression filled with a mother's love.

Rose looked from Lydia to Davy's hopeful expression. "What about —"

"George?" Lydia offered. Rose nodded. "He won't be a problem. I have full custody of Davy, and he has my permission to work here. I know Dr. Mackenzie would not allow him to do anything dangerous."

Not feeling she had the authority to say yes or no, Rose went to the connecting door. "Doctor, can you please come out here?"

A few moments later, Hunter emerged. "Yes?" He noticed Davy and Lydia. "Hi."

"Doctor, Davy would like his job back, if that's okay with you." Rose noticed that Davy still clung to his mother's hand. For moral support, no doubt.

Hunter smiled at the boy. "As far as I'm concerned, he never quit."

"Ya mean it, Doc?"

"Like I said. I don't remember you telling me you quit." Hunter put the emphasis on *you*.

Davy's face broke into a wide grin. "Cool. Can I go see Sadie?"

"May I," his mother corrected.

"Yeah. May I?"

Hunter looked at Lydia. She nodded. "You sure can. She's been wondering where you've been."

Before anyone could blink, Davy was out

the door and on a dead run toward the wolf's shelter. The three adults laughed.

"Thank you, Hunter," Lydia said, still watching her son as he raced across the yard. "All he's talked about since George dragged him out of here is that wolf."

Hunter shook his head. "I don't know how he did it, but he's developed a relationship with her that is beyond anything I've ever seen or heard tell of between a wild animal and a human."

Lydia winked. "That's my boy." Then she grew serious. "He's truly amazing. I've seen him feed a female deer from his hand the first time he approached her. I've seen squirrels sit on his shoulder and eat nuts. They seem to sense that he's special and would never harm them. He communicates with them somehow, like they have a silent language all their own. He loves all animals, and I would never come between him and that love. No matter what George says, Davy can stay here as long as you want him here. I've already told George to stay out of it."

Hunter knew that George wouldn't stay out of it, that he'd find a way to stop Davy and perhaps even close the wildlife refuge. He'd be living in a fool's paradise if he thought otherwise. "Thanks, Lydia. Davy is a good worker and a great asset to this place. He's got a job here as long as he cares to have one." *Or until George makes good his threat.*

Hunter watched as Rose cleared her desk of the remains of the lunch he'd brought for them from Terri's Tearoom on his way through town. The afternoon sun flashed a beam of light through the glass in the front door and highlighted the red in Rose's hair. He had all he could do not to grab a handful and let the strands sift through his fingers.

"What?"

He blinked and realized that she'd caught him staring at her. "I . . . uh . . ." He fumbled for words and snatched at the first thing that entered his head. "You have a little mustard on your face, right there."

He pointed at his own cheek. She wiped at it but missed it. He reached across the desk and removed the mustard with the pad of his thumb. The slight physical contact brought to life all the emotions he'd been suppressing since he'd first laid eyes on her. Immediately he pulled back.

"Thanks," she whispered as if in a trance, while running her fingertips over the spot he'd just touched.

Quickly averting his gaze from her mesmerizing, beautiful eyes, he wiped the mustard on his thumb on a paper napkin and dropped it in the wastebasket beside the desk. He wanted to bolt into the safer sanctuary of the back room, but didn't want it to look like he was running away from her either. Instead, trying for casual, he picked up his soda can and took a sip.

What he needed was some neutral ground, ground that wouldn't bring to life any sexual innuendos or get him thinking about things that could only end dangerously for both of them.

"How's the lion cub doing? Is he still eating for you?" He knew very well how the cub was doing. He'd checked on him daily. But he was grasping at straws to keep the conversation in an area that didn't end up with him paying more attention to the speaker than the subject.

Rose laughed. "He's doing great, but not because I'm feeding him. Give the credit to Davy. He has some closet secret to getting these animals to do whatever he wants them to do. He's got the cub eating dry food already." She leaned back in her chair. "So how did your house calls go yesterday? What with all the excitement, I never got a chance to ask."

It pleased Hunter that she had taken an interest in the business. His old receptionist put in her eight hours, could have cared less about the business or the patients and couldn't get out of there fast enough at the end of the day. He'd always suspected that, unlike Rose, she really didn't care for animals.

"Pretty smoothly, until I got to Sam Watkins' farm. His daughter thought Missy Peggy, the pig she's grooming as a 4-H project, was sick, so the girl brought her into the house. Then they couldn't find her. Turns out, unbeknownst to anyone, Peggy was messing with one of the males, and she'd picked Mrs. Watkins' closet to give birth to six little piglets — right inside her new suitcase."

Rose laughed out loud. Hunter caught his breath as the sound washed over him like a warm summer shower. He coughed and straightened in the chair.

"That reminds me . . ." Rose sobered and then glanced at him as if hesitant about going on.

"Reminds you of what?" he prompted.

She leaned on her forearms and smiled. "My friend Beth told me about the time her mom was putting away clean linens in the bathroom. The phone rang, and she went to answer it, then got sidetracked doing something else. When she got back, their cat had had kittens right on top of the clean laundry." She giggled and sounded like the younger girl she must have been when Beth related the story.

But what really caught Hunter's attention was the way Rose's face lit up when she spoke about her friend. Her eyes sparkled and took on a life that, until now, he hadn't realized had been missing from her expression. He already knew Rose was beautiful, but now, a brilliant radiance shined through. Even though he wished he'd been the reason for this change in her and not her friend, he wanted that look to never go away. If talking about Beth put it there, then perhaps more talk of her could keep it there.

"So, tell me more about Beth."

She stiffened, then avoiding his gaze, began hastily clearing away the leftovers from their lunch. "There's really not much to tell."

"You said she used to live in the Johnson house on the edge of town. I grew up here, and I can't recall her at all." He set his soda can on the desk. "How old was she?"

"About my age. Are you finished with your sandwich?"

He rolled up the end of his sub in the

paper it had come in and handed it to her. "Did she live there long?"

"She never said." She held up the remains of a dill spear. "Do you want your pickle?"

He shook his head. "Does she have any relatives in the area?"

She shrugged. "Hand me your napkin."

Hunter gave her the napkin, and she crumpled it and threw it in the wastepaper basket.

"Did you inquire to see?"

She shook her head.

What had started out as a casual conversation had now caught Hunter's interest. It had become obvious to Hunter from her clipped responses that Rose was being evasive. Why? And what was she hiding?

"Rose, why —"

"Are you done with your soda?" She reached for the can.

Hunter rescued it just in time to keep it from being thrown in the trash.

It suddenly occurred to him that he'd been asking question that were really none of his business. It's no wonder she had shut down. Since she didn't want to talk about Beth, he'd let it drop, but not before he apologized. "I'm sorry if it sounded like I was prying. I didn't mean to." When she didn't answer, he prodded her. "Rose?"

Please, just let it go! She didn't want to talk about Beth. Not because she didn't miss her friend every day, but because talking about Beth brought to mind the secret she was carrying under her heart, a secret she hadn't shared with Hunter. A secret that in a few weeks would begin to become very apparent, leaving her with one choice . . . to tell him.

Desperate to bring a halt to his questions, she checked her watch. "Mrs. Wright is due any minute with her cat Fluffy. I need to get her file out before she gets here, and I'm sure you have things to do in the back to get ready." She stood, went to the filing cabinet, pulled open the drawer and began rifling through the folders ostensibly looking for Mrs. Wright's file.

From the corner of her eye, she saw Hunter get to his feet, but he paused. For a long moment he studied her, and then finally, he went into the back room.

Rose breathed a deep sigh and collapsed into her desk chair. *Nice going, Rose. Now all you've done is make him more curious. You should have just answered his questions. He doesn't know about the babies and talking about Beth wasn't going to let your secret out.*

A thought suddenly struck her. Exactly why was she keeping her pregnancy a secret from Hunter anyway? In the beginning it was because she'd been afraid he wouldn't hire an expectant mother, but she'd more than proved her worth to him as an employee. After that, there just never seemed a good time to introduce the subject. Or so she'd told herself. In actuality, she'd had several opportunities to tell him.

But she had continued to keep her silence. Why? It wasn't as if being pregnant would inhibit her from doing her job. So what was it? Could it be that the prospect of him finding out about the babies would negate any chance of Hunter seeing her as more than just an employee? Or could it be something more? Had she done the very thing she'd been telling herself not to do? Had she fallen in love with the one man who would never want to get involved with her because starting a relationship with her meant taking on the responsibility of a ready-made family?

CHAPTER 7

Since yesterday over lunch, when Hunter had started quizzing her about Beth, Rose had thought a lot about her reasoning for not telling Hunter about the babies. Since there was no hope of ever having a relationship with him, and she had nothing but her job and a free apartment to lose, and she didn't believe either of those possibilities would come to pass, she'd finally made up her mind. Keeping the existence of the twins from him was just getting too hard and certainly would not get any easier as time went on. Today would be the day she divulged her secret and let the chips fall where they may. Better she tell him now than wait until he found out by accident or when she started to show and had to tell him.

And if she did lose her job, there were always other jobs. And if she couldn't find another position and though it went against everything in her to do so, she could always go on public assistance until she did. Although she'd really come to love working with animals, having Davy around and interacting with the people of Carson . . . with the exception of the community's mayor.

However, never seeing Hunter, even though she knew nothing could come of it, would be the hardest part of leaving. Even an idiot knew what the bottomless feeling that attacked her tummy whenever he walked into a room or the way her heart raced at his touch meant. She'd done exactly what she'd cautioned herself against. She'd fallen in love with Hunter Mackenzie.

How could she not have? He was everything any woman could want: kind, gentle, a good listener, a friend, and a darn good cook. In short, he was too good to be true.

Just her luck. All her life Rose had been too late for one thing or another. She'd been born the week after her father had walked out on her mother. As a result, she never knew the man who helped give her life. She'd come home from school mere hours after her mother had run out on her, leaving her to face the social service people and a parade of foster homes alone, frightened and confused.

This was one time she would get the jump on Fate. She'd tell Hunter about the twins and do it right now.

Determined, she clicked the answering machine on, then pushed her chair back from the desk and marched into the back room. "Hunter, I need to speak to you about . . ." The room was empty.

Odd. She hadn't seen him come through the front. She checked behind the cages and in the storeroom, but both were empty.

Then she noticed the back door wide open. She stepped through it into the yard Hunter used to exercise the dogs that required a prolonged stay at the clinic. Seated at the picnic table on the far side of the yard was Hunter, his gaze fastened on Hawks Mountain in the distance. As she grew closer, she realized he probably didn't see the lush green peaks, but instead was deep in thought.

"Hunter?"

He jumped and then blinked as if bringing his thoughts back to the here and now. "Rose." He said her name almost vacantly. Then he blinked again. This time his eyes seemed more focused. "Do I have an appointment waiting?"

The discussion she'd planned to have with him fled from her mind. She sat next to him. "No. You don't have another until Grace Raymond brings in her little Pekinese for her checkup." She sat next to him and laid a hand on his arm. "Is there something wrong?'

He laughed without humor. "Not a thing unless you count the fact that any moment now George could lower the boom and get his dearest wish in the world . . . closing the wildlife refuge." He ran his hand through his tousled brown hair. From the unkempt look of it, that hadn't been the first time he'd done that today.

"Wanna talk about it?"

Again that humorless laugh. "I'm not sure talking will solve anything." He shook his head and sighed, an empty, helpless sound. "George is determined to close the refuge down. I don't know what to do, short of getting rid of the animals, and I refuse to do that."

Rose's heart twisted. Everything in her wanted to solve his problem and remove the worry lines from his face, but like Hunter, she had no answers. "Maybe he'll give up from the sheer exhaustion of fighting you." Even as she said the words, they sounded futile.

Hunter forced a smile. "Thanks, but George isn't the giving-up type. Unfortunately, I know him all too well. He's like a hound on the scent of a fox. He'll keep at it until he succeeds."

The pain in Hunter's voice seeped into Rose. She choked back the emotion threatening to fill her throat. No reminders were needed for her to understand how much Hunter loved this business and the animals he cared for, wild and domestic. It would devastate him to lose them.

The kind of determination she'd called on to survive in foster care blossomed inside her. She couldn't . . . no, *wouldn't* let that arrogant windbag take away one of the most important things in Hunter's life. George Collins may be determined, but he'd never come up against Rose Hamilton at her best.

She squeezed Hunter's fingers. "Then we'll make sure he doesn't succeed. We'll just have to put our heads together and beat him at his own game."

The determination filling her voice must have registered with Hunter. When he turned to look at her, some of the worry that had marked his face with deep frown lines had eased.

"What did I ever do to deserve you in my life?"

But I'm not in your life, not really, not like I'd love to be.

Then he cupped her cheek in his hand. For a long moment, their gazes locked. All thought of their dilemma and the animals vanished from her mind. An uncontrollable eddy of emotions sucked her into a vortex of sudden desire. Her gaze shifted to his mouth. Unbidden thoughts accosted her. If he kissed her, would she be able to stop him . . . or herself? Would she want to?

Though Rose knew no good could come of this, she was helpless to stop the yearning growing inside her for Hunter's kiss. She tilted her head back and gazed into is eyes.

As if sucked down by a wave's undertow, Hunter became lost in her blue eyes. *My God, she is so beautiful, so absolutely beautiful.* He leaned toward her, anticipating the feel of her lips against his. Her warm, sweet breath brushed across his face, heightening the desire rising in him. He wanted to kiss her. He *had* to kiss her.

Very slowly he closed the distance between them. Then it happened . . . her mouth touched his. Lightly at first, like the caress of a butterfly's wing, so soft it almost wasn't there.

He slid closer to her and pulled her to him. Without conscious thought, he intensified the kiss, silently voicing all the frustration of weeks of keeping his distance from her. Her female curves melded with his masculine angles as if she'd been fashioned for him and only him.

He was half aware that her arms now encircled his neck, pulling his mouth down harder on hers. He'd fallen into a pool of heated sensuality, and it was rapidly closing over his head, blocking out rationality. Soft, incoherent moans emanated from her.

He knew he should pull away, stop it before they passed the point of no return. But he couldn't. Now that he had her in his arms, he never wanted to let her go.

Honk! Honk!

Vaguely, in the back of his mind he heard the noise, but the cloud of sensuality that had enveloped him wouldn't let it register. Something told him he needed to listen, but something even stronger told him not to release Rose because this might never happen again. He tightened his grip.

Honk! Honk!

This time the strident blast of a horn broke through the sensual stupor. Both of them jumped back, as though they'd been caught necking under the athletic field bleachers by the school principal. Dazed, Hunter sprang to his feet and quickly climbed over the picnic table bench.

Honk! Honk!

The horn blasted again. He looked toward the front of the building and could make out just the front of the semi that delivered the feed once a week.

"Sorry," he mumbled and with one wistful glance at Rose, he walked quickly toward the back door, leaving Rose sitting on the bench looking as bewildered as he felt.

Hunter ground the ancient truck's transmission into second gear, let out the clutch, then stepped down hard on the gas. "Come on, Bessie. You can do it."

With his coaching, the truck's engine whined, but it took the hill with little trouble. The truck may have been old, but he'd had it since he'd opened his veterinary practice, and, with his gentle care, it was in pretty good shape. Having become attached to it, Hunter refused to replace it until it fell apart around him. After shifting into third gear, he tried to concentrate on the landscape around him. Anything was better than thinking about the kiss he'd shared with Rose hours before.

But it was no use. His blood still sang through his veins with the memory. God, but she'd tasted so good and felt so good against him. How would he ever function with her there every day reminding him that he wanted more, much more of Rose Hamilton?

But you can't have more, his conscience reminded him. *Not without all the responsibilities that go with a relationship.*

And getting involved with Rose would not be a simple matter of dates and perhaps a little sex thrown in. He felt it in his bones that casual affairs were not her thing. Oddly, when he thought about Rose, what really scared him was that a casual affair didn't appeal to him either.

What really scared the bejesus out of him was that sometimes he'd lie in bed at night and think about her. Then other insane thoughts would sneak into his mind, things like a little house with a picket fence, much like the one Beth had described to Rose.

The thought of Beth's house gave him an idea. Ever since he'd left Sam Watkins' farm, he'd been dreading coming face-to-face with Rose again. Not because he wasn't longing to see her. He just needed time. Time to think this out. Time to figure out what to do about the crazy feelings he'd been experiencing since the kiss they'd shared. He decided to take the long way home, past the Johnson house.

Ever since Rose had told him about it, it

had been niggling at the back of his mind. The more he thought about Rose's description of the place, the more certain he'd been that no such home existed. At least not the way Beth had described it to Rose. This was the perfect opportunity to put his mind at ease, not to mention the perfect excuse not to go back to the office. Following his impulsive change of mind, he swung the truck in a wide U-turn and headed back toward the road that led past the house.

A few minutes later, he rounded a sharp curve and the road leveled off before making the dip that connected Santee Ridge Road with the main road into Carson. He turned onto the road and almost at once a house came into view. Or at least what was left of a house.

Hunter pulled his pickup into the weed-infested driveway and came to a stop. For a long time he sat in the truck staring at the place. The siding had passed the point of needing paint a long time ago. Two remaining shutters hung by a single hinge from the window frame and several more had been piled haphazardly against the house. Grass and weeds choked out most of the driveway and nearly hid the house, and large patches of missing shingles dotted the roof. If roses had ever grown in this yard, they'd long since seen their last days.

He turned to the mailbox peeking out from the tall stand of weeds near the road, barely visible letters scrawled across its side. The only letter still decipherable was an L. He struggled to recall what Rose had said Beth's last name was.

Lawson? Logan? Lawman? Lawrence? Yes, Lawrence.

Suddenly a memory accosted him. A memory that he'd tucked away as unimportant at the time. It had been two days before Halloween, and he'd been driving by with a bunch of his teenaged friends. He'd seen a dirty little girl in a ragged dress sitting in the front yard digging in a pile of dirt with a spoon and putting the dirt in a tin can. He remembered wondering what she was doing out there in her bare feet and with no coat in October.

Hunter's friend had slowed the car down almost to a standstill because this was supposedly the house where the town "hooker" lived, and being young, inquisitive boys, they wanted to get a peek at her. Just then a woman in an open bathrobe and smeared makeup had emerged through the front door and ushered a man out on the porch. He'd stopped for a moment and handed her some bills. She'd kissed him and waved as he'd gotten into his car, then she'd turned to the child and yelled, "Get inside."

The boys had whooped and hollered and driven off, and Hunter had dismissed the incident from his mind. After all, she was just a little girl. Now, he had to wonder if that little girl had been Beth Lawrence.

Slowly, he slid from the truck and made his way to the back of the house. There, in the middle of the backyard, stood a giant maple tree. One of the lower branches extended out from the trunk at almost a ninety degree angle. He walked over and stood under it, then looked up. The branch held no telltale scars of once holding the tire swing that Beth had described to Rose.

Had that whole story Beth told Rose been just a figment of her imagination? A story made up to be what Beth would have liked her life to have been like? His heart twisted for that little barefoot girl and for the teenager who'd had to invent a decent childhood so she wouldn't have to face the memory of the nightmare it had actually been.

With a heavy heart Hunter went back to his truck. He started it and turned to back out of the driveway. Then he spotted a For Sale sign peeking out from between the white lacy flowers of a large growth of

Queen Anne's Lace. He shook his head. Anyone who bought this place would have a major renovation project on their hands.

Then, with no clear reason for doing so, he pulled a small notepad from the glove box and jotted down the phone number on the sign.

All the way back to the office, Hunter tried to make up his mind if he'd tell Rose what he'd found. Should he destroy Beth's dream and along with it Rose's trust in her friend by telling Rose what he'd seen at the Johnson place, what Beth's *idyllic* life had really been like?

He recalled the look in Rose's eyes when she'd related Beth's description of the house and her life. It didn't take a genius to figure out that Rose had adopted that life as her own dream, too. If he destroyed Beth's fantasy world, he'd destroy Rose's as well.

Did he want to do that? More to the point, *could* he do that?

CHAPTER 8

Rose stood in front of the mirror in the bathroom looking at her nude profile. She ran her hand over her surprisingly flat stomach. From her nursing experience on the obstetric wing of the last hospital she'd worked in, she knew that some women carrying twins went as far as their seventeenth week before they started showing. However, once they did, it seemed that they expanded very quickly. Thankfully, she appeared to be one of the late bloomers and, aside from the nausea, which had subsided weeks ago, none of the normal symptoms of frequent urination, increased appetite and heartburn had manifested themselves yet either.

But she'd need to find an obstetrician soon. She hadn't had a checkup since she left her old job, which was when her supervisor found out about the babies.

She grabbed a towel and wrapped it around her body, then headed into the bedroom to get dressed for work. *Work.* That one word had the power to resurrect something Rose had been trying to put to the back of her mind since yesterday.

She flopped down on the bed and stared at the ceiling. Why in God's name had she let Hunter kiss her? Even worse, why had she responded?

Because you love him, and because you've been wanting him to kiss you for weeks.

But it's wrong. He doesn't want a family. So nothing can come of it.

Then why didn't you tell him about the babies?

She hesitated, searching for a reason. *Well, because . . . because I got distracted when I found he was worried about the mayor taking the animals away.*

Pitiful excuse. And what about when he came back from his house call? You couldn't wait to get out of the office and into the safety of your apartment.

She sat up, clutching the towel around her. That's exactly what she'd done. She'd had the afternoon to think about what had happened on the picnic bench, and while she'd loved it, she knew it had been a taste of something akin to Eve's forbidden fruit. And it only made it harder to be with him and not be able to . . .

She stood and threw the towel to the side, then began pulling clothes from the closet. Why was she torturing herself? Hunter didn't want the responsibility of a family, and she came with one built-in, so to speak. End of story.

The question of a relationship with Hunter was moot, and Rose didn't think he'd fire her because she was pregnant. So she really had no reason not to tell him about the twins. It was time.

She owed him a meal, so she'd invite him to dinner tonight and tell him then.

Later that morning, Davy came through the office door, his face grim. "Hey, Miss Rose."

From experience, Rose knew it took a lot to erase the perpetual smile from Davy's mouth. Most times, on the rare occasions when it did happen, it had something to do with the animals. "Hi, Davy. Why so sad?"

He shuffled his feet on the linoleum floor and glanced at her, then back at the floor. "Mom says Dad might close the refuge and get rid of all the animals. Is that so?"

"I'm afraid so, but Doc and I are trying to find a way to stop him."

He flopped down in the chair beside her desk. "We should load everybody in town on the school buses and bring them all out here and show them that none of the animals will hurt them." He fiddled with something in his lap while he talked.

"Whatcha got there?"

His face brightened some. "It's a friendship collar I made for Sadie." He held it up. "Think she'll like it?"

The collar was fashioned of braided colored ribbons. "It's lovely, Davy. Very stylish. I'm sure she'll love it, mostly because it came from you, but you'd better ask Doc first. Okay?"

"Okay." That seemed to take the edge off his worry about what his father was trying to do. "I'm gonna go show it to her before I start feeding the animals." He jumped to his feet and dashed from the building, letting the door slam behind him.

With a smile teasing at her lips, Rose watched him go, wishing she could forget about what George had up his sleeve as easily as the boy.

"Who was that?"

Rose jumped at the sound of Hunter's voice. "Davy. He's made a friendship collar for Sadie and ran off to show it to her."

Hunter laughed. "Maybe we should get him to make one for George."

Rose frowned. That wasn't the type of collar she had in mind for the troublesome mayor. If only it were that simple to change George's mind. Then she recalled what Davy had suggested about bringing the townspeople out there to prove the animals were harmless.

"Hunter, I need to talk to you." About more than just the mayor.

He held up his medical bag. "Can it wait until later? I'm on my way out. One of Catherine Daniels' thoroughbreds has gone into labor, and she's in trouble."

"Sure. How about over dinner? My place? Around seven or so? After all, I owe you one."

He grinned. "It's a date." Then he winked and hurried out the door. "Cancel the rest of my appointments for today," he called over his shoulder. "I should be back by seven, but I'll call if I'm going to be late."

She waved and then grabbed her pen and a legal pad and started writing. Since Hunter was gone and no patients would be interrupting her, Rose could spend the rest of the day working out the plan to implement Davy's suggestion.

By the time she shut down the office and went home to start dinner, she had a very viable plan in place, one that she thought Hunter would go for and that could stop George Collins once and for all.

146

Now, all she had to do was make sure her nerve didn't desert her when it came time to tell him about the pregnancy.

Cooking had never been one of Rose's strong points, but she found she couldn't go wrong with the help of Newman's Own Sockarooni Marinara Sauce, a tossed salad and an already seasoned loaf of garlic bread she would just toss in the oven and heat up while the spaghetti cooked. The table was set, the oven was heating in preparation for putting in the bread, the salad chilling in the fridge and the sauce simmering away on the stove. She just wished that telling Hunter her secret could be prepared for as easily.

Hunter's truck had pulled into the yard twenty minutes ago. He must be showering away the aftermath of delivering a colt. She knew from working in hospital delivery rooms that that was not something he'd want to bring to the dinner table.

Rose glanced at the clock. Six forty-five. At seven she'd put the spaghetti water on to boil. That would give her fifteen minutes to fret over what she would be talking to Hunter about tonight, and it wasn't just the plans to stop George. What she had to tell him after they'd discussed her plan was what had been causing her stomach to roil since that afternoon.

Having this dinner here, in this intimate atmosphere, probably hadn't been the smartest idea for someone who was trying to distance herself from the man who would be sharing the meal with her. But, as silly as it sounded, she'd decided she'd feel much more comfortable discussing the babies in familiar surroundings. The problem with that being, if things didn't go well, she'd look really silly walking out of her own house. Then again, at that point, it wouldn't matter much.

To keep her hands busy and her mind occupied, she fussed with the table, straightening silverware and lining it up just so, making sure the glasses were positioned at the tip of the knife, refolding the napkins and removing the candles because they looked too romantic. Then she did it all again. By the time she was ready to rearrange the table for the third time, a knock sounded on the door at the foot of the stairs.

"Come in," she called, taking a deep breath to fortify herself for the evening ahead of her.

The door squeaked open, and then closed quietly. Then footsteps sounded on the stairs. She swallowed and waited for that bottomless dip in her stomach that happened every time she came face to face with this man.

"Hi. I brought wine." Hunter stood at the top of the stairs holding up a bottle of red wine.

This time, her stomach didn't dip. It did its own version of the tarantella. A pale blue Izod hugged his well-developed chest and biceps and if his jeans were any snugger, he wouldn't be able to walk.

God help her!

Quickly, she turned back to the stove and flipped on the burner beneath the pot of spaghetti water, then shoved the bread in the hot oven. A wave of heat washed her face as she closed the oven door.

"Red wine is perfect to go with the spaghetti." She turned to him again, hoping he'd interpret the flush she could feel invading her face as a result of the hot stove. "How did you guess?"

"I smelled the sauce when I got out of the truck." He came to where she stood beside the stove and peered over her shoulder into the pot of simmering sauce. "*Mmm.* Smells great."

Too close.

Rose stepped away and grabbed the handle of the refrigerator for balance. "Why don't you open the wine and pour yourself a glass while I get the salad on the table?" Rummaging through the silverware drawer, she extracted a corkscrew and handed it to him.

He frowned. "That's right. I forgot that you don't drink."

She forced a smile. "No reason you can't." *You're not pregnant.*

That thought reminded her of what she had to tell Hunter later that evening. But she pushed it to the back of her mind. First she wanted to run her plan to save his beloved animals by him.

While Hunter poured the wine, Rose put the salad and dressing on the table, then the timer went off to signal the spaghetti was done. She drained it and added the sauce, then put it on the table in a large serving bowl and went back to the kitchen area to get the bread from the oven and slice it. All the time she was increasingly conscious of Hunter's eyes following her every move.

Despite Rose's apprehensions, dinner proved to be very pleasant. They talked about the patients who'd come through the clinic the previous day, and Hunter's house call to deliver the foal, a beautiful little pinto filly.

They were finishing dessert, a store-bought apple pie with vanilla ice cream, and sipping after-dinner decaf coffee. Hunter looked relaxed and content, and Rose decided it was a good time to approach him with her plan.

"Hunter, I was thinking today about George Collins —"

Frowning, he held up a hand. "Please, don't spoil a lovely dinner with talk of him."

Leaning forward, she rested her hand on his. "Please. Hear me out."

He was silent for a moment, then one corner of his mouth quirked up in a half smile. "Okay. What about George?"

Gathering her thoughts, she leaned back in her chair. "I have an idea that . . . actually, it sort of started with something Davy said . . . that might just get George off your back."

His expression changed to one of immediate interest. "Keep talking."

"Well, what if we had an open house? Let the townsfolk come and see that the animals aren't dangerous." Words spewed from her as she attempted to get the entire idea out there before he could make a judgment. "We could have hot dogs and games for the kids and maybe even let them pet some of the baby animals. If they see for themselves that there's no danger, then maybe George will be outvoted on the town council, and he'll find someone else to antagonize." The room went deadly silent. Hunter didn't say anything. He just sat there fiddling with his spoon and staring at the table.

Rose waited.

Still he just sat there.

"Well? What do you think?"

He said nothing.

He hated the idea. Her heart sank.

Suddenly, he vaulted from the chair, rounded the table and swept her into his arms in a bear hug. "You're a genius. It's so simple. Why didn't I think of this?" He swung her around, and then stopped abruptly, set her on the floor and before she could catch her breath, he kissed her. Hard. On the mouth.

It all happened so suddenly that she clung to his neck to keep her balance. Then the kiss stopped being one of thanks for coming up with a plan to save the refuge and turned into one of a man kissing a woman, a woman he didn't want to let go.

Hunter hadn't intended for the kiss to be more than a thank you for her great idea, but as soon as his mouth closed over hers, he couldn't stop himself from deepening it, savoring her in the way he'd wanted to for weeks.

He pulled her closer, loving the way they fit together from head to toe. In the back of his mind he knew he should stop this craziness before it got out of hand. Then she melted against him, tightened her hold on his neck and cupped the back of his head in her palm, imprisoning his mouth against hers.

The need in him had swelled and intensified, drowning out the little voice cautioning him against doing something they'd both regret come morning. As if he'd been sucked down by an invisible whirlpool, Hunter lost all sense of time, of space. He could do nothing but feel.

Wrapped in a sensual daze, he bent and lifted her body against him, then walked into her bedroom and kicked the door closed behind them.

Hours later, Rose lay wrapped in Hunter's arms in her big double bed, basking in the wonder of what had just happened. As Hunter's breath feathered her hair, she smiled contentedly. She'd never before felt so complete, so totally at ease with life . . . except for the one thing that would make it perfect. The time had come to clear her conscience of its secret.

She snuggled closer. "Hunter?"

"Hmm?"

He'd been so quiet, for a moment she'd thought he'd fallen asleep. The hand that had been smoothing the skin of her bare shoulder had stopped moving, and his breath had slowed to a leisurely pace.

"We need to talk."

She waited for a reply.

"Hmm. Wha' about?" The fog of impending sleep cloaked his voice. He snuggled deeper into the pillow, his face buried in her hair.

Taking a deep breath, she chewed on her bottom lip, searching for the words, then released it and swallowed hard. She pulled from his embrace and propped herself up on one bent arm. Unable to look at him, her gaze dropped to the blankets barely covering their nude bodies. Her nerveless fingers toyed with the hem of the blanket. Bending her head forward, she used the long, unbound tresses of her hair as a temporary place of refuge while she gathered her nerve.

Seconds stretched out into minutes. A knot of dread began to form in her belly as she finally blurted out the words she'd been

working so hard to form. "I'm pregnant . . .
with twins."

CHAPTER 9

Rose stared out the open office door at Sadie as she limped around the exercise pen with Davy beside her monitoring every step she took. The summer sun glistening off the boy's shock of unruly black hair took a backseat to his grin. Sadie's leg was getting better every day, thanks to Davy's devotion to the animal. Unfortunately, the better Sadie got, the sooner Davy would lose his friend to the wolf preserve.

But Rose's mind wasn't really on the wolf or Davy or the view. Instead, it kept replaying the night before. She couldn't believe that Hunter had slept through her confession about being pregnant. It had taken all she had to tell him, and he never heard her. For a long time, she'd laid beside him thinking about how she would have to summon up her courage again in the morning. But she was saved that stress. The next morning, Hunter was gone.

He came into the office late and mumbled a quick *Good Morning* in her direction, then disappeared into the back. Since then, he'd been acting strange. Not distant or angry or regretful. Just . . . evasive. Effectively keeping himself busy with his patients and not making eye contact with her whenever he was forced to come into the office.

Confusion fogged Rose's mind. Was he embarrassed? Did he regret making love last night? Had it been a one-night stand for him? She couldn't tell. One thing she did conclude, he did not want to talk about it, and he had been going out of his way to avoid a situation that would enable a conversation. And if he didn't want to talk, how could she tell him about the babies without tackling him and sitting on his chest to make him listen?

"She'll be fine, Ida. Just make sure when you give her a marrowbone that the hole isn't big enough for her to get her lower jaw through."

Hunter led Ida Simmons and her Golden Retriever, Lulu, out of the back room. Mrs. Simmons looked more shook-up than Lulu, who had come in with a marrowbone trapped on her lower jaw behind her canine teeth. The dog had been quite docile, but Mrs. Simmons had been hysterical. It had taken Hunter a half an hour to calm the owner before he could begin to remove the bone.

"Thank you so much, Dr. Mackenzie." She held her hand up as if to block her next words from the dog's hearing. "Between you and me, I think Lulu has seen her last marrowbone." Then she put her hand over her heart. "I just couldn't take another episode like this." She paid her bill and led Lulu from the building.

Hunter didn't have another patient for an hour, so Rose turned to him, determined to talk to him at last. She opened her mouth to speak, and the phone rang. Seemed she just couldn't catch a break.

Sighing, she picked up the receiver. "Paws and Claws Clinic. How may I help you?" Pause. "Yes, Mr. . . . I'll tell Dr. . . . You need to calm down, sir." She threw Hunter a pleading look.

He took the phone from her. "This is Dr. Mackenzie." He listened for a moment. "Is she standing?" Another pause. "All right. Stay calm. Keep her on her feet, and I'll be there in a few minutes. You understand, Fred? Do not let her lay down." He hung up the phone and began stripping his lab coat off as he hurried into the back room. A few moments later he emerged carrying his bag. "Cancel my appointments for the rest of the day. Fred Tyson's mare has colic. I'm not sure how long I'll be." And he was gone.

Rose stared helplessly at the empty doorway and listened to the roar of Hunter's truck as it careened out of the driveway.

As Hunter drove, he thought about the night before and the implications of what he'd foolishly done. No way in heaven or on earth did he regret making love to Rose. The whole experience had been . . . incredible, earthmoving. Never in his life had he felt more fulfilled, more content, more alive. But —

But? What's your problem, Mackenzie?

He'd slept with his employee. That's the problem. To add to that, he had no idea what to do about it. He didn't want the entanglements of a relationship. He didn't even want a relationship. But making love to Rose was like letting an alcoholic take one drink and then telling him he couldn't have anymore. All he'd been able to think about since he left her that morning had been the next time. But there couldn't be a next time.

Rose wasn't the kind of woman a man played with then discarded. She was the forever type, the type that wanted little houses with white picket fences, rose gardens and tire swings. And Hunter just wasn't ready for that kind of commitment or the responsibilities that went along with it. That meant never again letting this happen with Rose.

Just the thought of never holding Rose again twisted Hunter's heart in his chest. He slammed his fist on the steering wheel and relished the pain that shot through his hand. Anything was better than the agony of what he knew he had to do about Rose.

Pleased that she'd at least managed to accomplish one of her goals for the day, Rose hung up the phone, jotted down the time and date of her appointment with the obstetrician in Charleston and then tore the sheet off and stuffed it in her purse. She'd been putting that off for far too long, and as a nurse, she knew that seeing a doctor on a regular basis while she was pregnant was critical to the babies' well-being.

No sooner had she hung up the phone than the problems facing her about telling Hunter assaulted her again. Not wanting to think about that right now, she pushed it to the back of her mind. However, it kept creeping back into her consciousness anyway.

Only one thing to do — find something to keep her busy, something that would occupy her time and her mind to the exclusion of all else. She thumbed through the file folders on her desk, but saw nothing needing her attention. They were all for patients that would be coming in tomorrow, so she'd only have to get them out again if she filed them.

As if heaven-sent, the door burst open and there, in the doorway, stood Davy Collins, hair askew, smears of dirt across his T-shirt and jeans, but his normally brilliant smile was missing.

"Hey, Miss Rose."

Happy for the distraction, Rose smiled at the boy. "Hey, Davy. What can I do for you?"

He lowered his gaze to his scuffed sneakers and shuffled his feet, a sure sign that something was troubling him.

Rising from her desk, Rose moved around it and guided Davy to one of the plastic chairs, then sat beside him. "Davy? What's the problem?" When he wasn't forthcoming, she squeezed his shoulder lightly. "Come on. You can tell me. We're buddies, right?"

He raised his gaze to meet hers and said sheepishly, "My mom told me I shouldn't bug you about it."

"About what?"

"About . . . well, about if you found a way to convince my dad not to close the doc's place." He gestured toward the animal compound buildings across the parking lot, his primary reason for asking obviously being Sadie.

Going to her desk, Rose retrieved the legal pad where she'd been making notes off and on all morning. She returned to her seat beside Davy. "As a matter of fact, I have an idea, and you gave it to me."

His eyes opened wide. "I did? Me?"

"Yup. And I spoke to Doc, and he's all for it. We're going to invite the town out here so they can see for themselves that the animals are harmless. We're gonna have an open house. Now, I need you to help come up with some ideas to make the day fun, but educational."

"All right!" Davy's eyes sparkled and that glowing smile had returned. The energy that normally kept his young body in perpetual motion burst forth. "Well, food's always a good idea. You know, like hot dogs and stuff."

Rose chuckled. Little boys and their stomachs. An inseparable combination of priorities. "Okay. I'll see if Granny Hawks can help us out in that department." She

162

jotted Granny Hawks' name next to the word *FOOD* that she'd printed in bold, capital letters to assure Davy of its importance on the list. "What else?"

His eyebrows furrowed in deep thought, almost meeting in the middle of his forehead. "Let me see . . ." He sat up straight. "I know. We need a petting place where people can feed the animals and pet them, and so the townsfolk can really see that the animals won't hurt them."

She'd thought of that as well, but she was unsure if actually putting the townspeople in the pens with the animals was a good idea. Rose didn't reply for a moment. Davy had a rapport with all the animals that went beyond explanation, but strangers were another thing altogether.

"Well, that's a great idea, but I think we need to speak to Doc Mackenzie about it first, just to make sure it's okay with him." Nevertheless, she scribbled *petting zoo* down on her notepad. Then an idea occurred to her. "How about we find someone with a camera, and they can take pictures of the people with the different animals?"

Davy almost flew out of his chair. "Yeah. Neat idea. My mom has a camera, and I bet she'd take pictures for us. Then I can get a picture of me and Sadie together."

The ideas continued to fly back and forth between them for the next hour. Some were keepers and some were discarded for lack of practicality or for some other reason. Soon, they had filled a whole page in Rose's legal pad with possible things they could do at the open house. If she could pull this off, the townspeople would have to accept that the animals weren't dangerous, and George wouldn't have a leg to stand on to close Hunter's refuge down.

Dusk had begun to settle over the valley by the time Hunter returned to the office. Because of the mountains on either side of the little town nestled between them, the days were shorter in Carson than most places in the summer. But the sunsets over the peaks were spectacular, picture-postcard quality.

Hunter's day had been long and exhausting. By the time he'd gotten the mare straightened out and out of danger, supper time had come and gone. His very bones ached with the need for some kicked-back-feet-up time. The one thing that would have made it nicer would have been someone to share it with. His gaze moved upward to the windows over the garage.

The lights from Rose's apartment spilled

out over the yard. For a time, he stood beside his truck looking up and wishing he dared go up there, share a cup of coffee with her and tell her about his day with the colicky mare. But that was not an option, not after last night.

He sighed and slammed the truck door, then unlocked the office and went inside to leave his bag. But he only got as far as Rose's desk when he collapsed, mostly out of sheer exhaustion, but somewhat out of regret that his life had suddenly turned lonely.

Sighing, he leaned against the chair back, then rolled his head to his left to stare out the window at the star-studded night sky. Immediately, Rose's scent, hidden in the chair's fabric, accosted him.

The smell brought last night to mind, vivid and all too real. The feel of her soft skin, the sweep of her silken hair against his flesh, the warmth of her breath on his lips.

Groaning, he sat up straight and buried his face in his hands. God help him, he wished the memories gone. He wished them consigned to the back of his mind along with those from the time when he'd been plunged into temporary parenthood.

Immediately, as if opening the door to tuck away last night's memories, others escaped. The long-ago memories of the days he'd had to be father and mother to Janice and Kenny slipped through the opening and accosted him as they hadn't in a very long time. As if it were only yesterday, the memories charged at him like an out-of-control freight train . . . and he was standing helpless in the middle of the tracks.

Hunter remembered sitting in the sheriff's office waiting for Kenny's release after Ben Ainsley had picked up him and some friends on Halloween night. It seems that Kenny and several other boys had decided it would be fun if they disassembled Sam Watkins' outhouse and reassembled it on the roof of his barn. Then there was the time Janice stayed out with her boyfriend three hours past curfew. Flat tire, she'd told him. Working three jobs to keep food in their bellies and a roof over their heads. Getting the news that he hadn't won that coveted scholarship to vet school and would have to pay for it out of his pocket with money he didn't have. Then working two jobs and trying to keep his grades up even though he was bone-tired most of the time.

By the time Janice and Kenny went to college, Hunter had had all he could take of parental fun and games. He'd been free for the first time in years, and he planned on never getting himself into that situation again. Now, here he was, falling for a woman who wouldn't and shouldn't settle for anything less than a gold band and a family.

Hunter rubbed at his throbbing temples. What he needed were a couple of aspirin, some hot food and a good night's sleep. Tomorrow, he'd worry about getting things straight with Rose and making sure she hadn't put any more meaning into last night than a night of lovemaking between two consenting adults. Nothing more.

Hunter locked the door and turned toward his house. The light in the window above the garage clicked off. He stood in the parking lot staring at the darkened window, his common sense telling him to let it go, his heart yearning to be up there with her.

Shoulders slumped and chin on his chest, he slowly made his way toward his house.

The sound of a truck coming up the driveway stopped his plodding progress and instantly shoved his troubles to the back of his mind.

CHAPTER 10

Hunter recognized the truck right away. Jerry Black drove the only shiny yellow 1987 Ford pickup in town. What he couldn't figure out was why Jerry was coming up his driveway at this time of night. The only possible answer — an injured animal. Jerry had to be the only other person in town with as soft a heart as Davy for the creatures in the forest. Probably his daddy's teachings throughout Jerry's childhood. Horace Black had loved all animals, wild or domesticated, and had instilled that love in his only son.

Stepping out of the path of the truck, Hunter waited until it came to a stop, and then strode to the driver's side window. "What brings you out here at this hour, Jerry?"

Jerry climbed down from the truck, his bib overalls opened at the sides and one strap hanging loose. "Got you a patient, Doc. Found her on the road south of town."

He sauntered to the back of the truck and dropped the tailgate. "Good thing she's just a young'un, or I'd have never been able to lift her into the truck."

Hunter peered into the darkened bed of the truck. Lying on its side, its front right leg at a weird angle, was a wild female hog which looked to be about four months old from her size and color. So much for that hot meal and warm bed.

Hunter turned to call Rose, but she was already standing behind him in her pajamas and robe. "I saw you from the window and thought you'd need me."

"I do. Her leg's fractured, and I'll need your help setting it. Jerry and I will get her inside. You go get dressed and meet me there. Jerry, I'd appreciate it if you'd stick around to help me move her into a pen after I've taken care of that leg."

Jerry nodded. "Glad to, Doc."

Without a backward glance to see if Rose was doing as he'd asked, Hunter hurried away toward the office to retrieve a stretcher on which to put the hog so he and Jerry could carry her inside. He knew he'd been a bit short with Rose, but the last thing he needed right now was her in her pj's, and his mind darting to places it shouldn't go if he wanted to keep his attention on treating the injured animal.

Fatigue dogged Rose the next day, clouding her ability to concentrate on the plans for the open house. The operation on the wild hog seemed to have taken forever, and she'd ended up getting just a couple hours of sleep. Her eyelids felt like they had lead weights attached to them, and the four cups of decaf coffee she'd poured down her throat so far were doing nothing to help her condition improve.

Nevertheless, with the open house looming closer each day, she had no option but to push on, making calls, arranging for tents to be delivered and set up, making preparations for the pictures with the animals, talking with Granny Jo about the food, and arranging with a printer in Charleston to do posters to hang around town. When she'd dropped Davy off that morning, Lydia had agreed to do the photos.

All Rose had left on her to-do list was to get the school to allow them to use the buses to bring people out to the refuge from town. Since George was on the school board and would never agree to let them use the buses, that plan presented a big problem.

She didn't want to leave it up to people to drive their own vehicles. For one thing, they'd never have room to park them all, but mostly because it made it too easy for them not to come. She'd planned to have the townspeople reserve their seats on the buses and then arrange to bring them out in scheduled shifts so there would be room for everyone. Once they made their reservations, it was way more likely that they'd see it through. But how did she get the use of the buses?

Only one person that Rose knew in Carson might have enough pull to get it done. Rose found the number in the files, and then punched it in. It rang twice before it was answered.

"Hello."

"Hi, Granny Jo. It's Rose at Dr. Mackenzie's office."

"Hello, dear." Then Granny Jo gasped. "Oh, goodness. Don't tell me I missed Jake's appointment."

Rose laughed. "No. His appointment isn't for a few weeks. I'm calling about a favor I wondered if you'd do for me." She told Granny Jo about the buses needed for the open house.

"I'd be happy to see if I can arrange it, dear. I'll call Asa Watkins. He's the school superintendent. He owes me a favor from back when he ran his car into my fence after . . . well, after he'd had a bit too much New Year's cheer a few years ago." She chuckled, then paused. "I meant to ask you before, but we got caught up in talking about hot dogs and such. Does George know what you're planning?"

"Not yet. I'm trying to keep him in the dark until it's too late for him to make a fuss about it." Rose sighed. "However, I'm afraid that as soon as the posters go up, I will be getting one of his raging phone calls."

Granny laughed again. "You no doubt will. But I sure wish I could be there to see the look on that old warthog's face when he hears about this."

They chatted for a few moments longer, and then hung up so Granny Jo could call Asa. Not more than thirty minutes later Granny Jo called back to tell Rose the school buses would be at her disposal for as long as she needed them.

Several days later, Rose had just gotten back from her appointment with the obstetrician in Charleston, when the phone rang. Tossing her purse on the desk and then turning off the answering machine, she hurried to pick up the receiver.

"Paws and Claws. How may I —"

"What's this crap about an open house

out there? Are you people nuts?"

Evidently, George had seen the posters Davy tacked up around town yesterday. "Mayor, I —"

"You're gonna turn those animals loose on the citizens of Carson? This is insane. Do you have any idea what could happen? People could be hurt, maybe killed."

"I can assure you —"

George's voice rose a few octaves. "You can't assure me of anything. These are wild beasts, unpredictable, untamed, capable of unspeakable things. How can you predict what they'll do?"

Knowing it was no use trying to reason with George Collins while he was in a raging fit, or any other time for that matter, Rose sat quietly and waited for his tirade to end. Resting her elbow on the desk and cupping her chin in her palm, she let him rant a while longer. However, *a while longer* turned into a five-minute litany of possible tragic events. All things both she and Hunter had heard innumerable times. Depending on the volume of his voice she either held the receiver to her ear or a few inches away to save her hearing while she doodled the word *idiot* on a notepad.

When he'd finally wound down to a low roar, she could take no more. "Thank you for drawing our attention to the possible problems, Mayor. I'll give Dr. Mackenzie your message, and I'm sure he will look into it." Then, not waiting for his reply, she hung up and pressed her thumbs against her throbbing temples. Though she'd fully expected this phone call, she hadn't expected it to be quite this bad.

Temples throbbing and the echo of George's voice still careening around her skull, Rose headed for the examination room in search of a towel to wet with cold water for her pounding head. As she walked toward the cabinet holding the clean towels, she thought she heard a soft, indistinguishable sound coming from inside it.

The door to the cabinet stood slightly ajar. Unsure of what she'd find, Rose very cautiously approached it and slowly opened the door the rest of the way. Her jaw dropped as she stared down into the cabinet.

Atop a pile of freshly laundered towels was Pansy. Snuggled into her belly were four tiny, damp kittens — three tabbies like their daddy Thomas and one orange tiger like its mom. Rose couldn't believe how tiny they were . . . mere inches long. She sat cross-legged on the floor and marveled at the sight of Pansy patiently laying there and allowing them to nurse, as if this wasn't her first time being a mom.

After a long while, the kittens seemed to have had their fill of mama's milk. Pansy began washing each of them with her tongue. While they squirmed and mewed, she continued her task until each kitten had been cleaned. Then she lay back and allowed them to curl into the curve of her tummy. Very quickly mama and the babies were asleep.

Rose got up and quietly left the room. She sat down at her desk and thought about Pansy's instinctive response to her new babies. Having worked in hospitals and seen new moms with their babies, Rose didn't doubt her instinctive response to the babies she carried. What she worried about was after they got home. Would she, like her mother, not have the fortitude to withstand the rigors of motherhood: dirty diapers, middle-of-the-night feedings, walking the floor with a sick child, seemingly never-ending chores that went hand in hand with infants?

Rose smiled and breathed deeply of the clean mountain air. They couldn't have ordered better weather for the festivities. The day of the open house had dawned bright, sunny and balmy. The emerald green mountains towered majestically against the cloudless, startlingly blue sky, and the sun hung above it all like a golden orb showering them with the blessing of its warmth and light.

Hopefully, a good omen for the day and its outcome.

Rose checked her watch. They still had a couple of hours before the buses started arriving with the Carsonites. Then she studied her clipboard to make sure she hadn't forgotten anything, and ticked off the attractions as she confirmed they were either already set up or in the process.

Granny Jo had arrived before anyone and already had delicious aromas wafting from the food tent at the far end of the parking lot. Jerry Black was helping Davy move some of the domesticated animals into the cordoned-off area they'd set up for the petting zoo. Far away from the petting zoo, on the other side of the parking lot, two larger, portable cages — one holding Boomer, the lion cub, and the other holding Sadie, Davy's wolf.

The wolf was not happy. She continually paced the confines of her cage, periodically glancing at Davy and whining. Occasionally, she howled mournfully. Rose assumed that Sadie didn't understand why her *buddy* wasn't playing with her and was trying to capture Davy's attention with her pitiful whimpers.

A second barrier had been erected around the cages to keep the visitors at a distance and to keep little hands from reaching into them. Rose and Hunter had agreed that, although they didn't see the animals as a risk, there was no sense giving George food for his gristmill.

"You've done a great job, Rose." Hunter had come to stand beside her and look out over the activity. "I don't know how you managed it in such a short time and with all the other work you have, but thank you. I hope it works."

Rose rested her hand on his forearm. "It will. Once the townspeople see that the animals are harmless, George won't have a leg to stand on."

He nodded, but she could see the doubt still lingering in his eyes. Truth be known, she had her own doubts about George seeing the light, but she kept them to herself.

"I'll take your word for it." Hunter smiled and rubbed his hands together. "So, what can I do?"

She glanced at her clipboard. "Can you bring out the wild hog? We'll put her in the pen next to Sadie's cage and safely inside the second fence." The hog, whom, much to Rose's amusement, Davy had named Rosebud, was mending nicely, and she was getting around remarkably well on her injured leg, even running from time to time. However, Hunter was keeping her until he could safely remove the soft cast before he turned her loose.

"You got it." He strode off toward the animal nursery.

Just then, Lydia came toward her carrying what appeared to be a very expensive camera. "My boss loaned it to me," she said in explanation to Rose's questioning stare. "He thought the pictures would be better quality than if I took them with my rinky-dink camera."

"That was very nice of —" A car driving into the parking area caught her attention. Hunter had stopped dead in his tracks and stared at the black Lexus.

Rose glanced at her watch. Aside from the fact that the visitors were to arrive on buses and not by car, it was still well before the start of the open house was scheduled.

"Who's that?" Lydia was staring at it as well. "I don't recognize the car."

"No idea." Rose checked her watch again. Then she noticed Hunter hurrying toward the car with a grin on his face. "Well,

Hunter seems to recognize whoever it is."

Both women watched until the car had come to a stop, and a man got out. A tall man with brown, wavy hair and a build that left no doubt he was a regular visitor to his local gym. His skintight jeans and white, Spiderman T-shirt molded his body like a second skin.

Lydia sighed appreciatively. "Oh my!"

"Do you recognize him, Lydia?"

Lydia closed her gaping mouth and shook her head. "I don't think I ever saw him before. With that build and that face, I kind of think I'd remember if had."

Hunter approached the newcomer with a broad smile and an outstretched hand. The man ignored Hunter's hand and instead swept him into a warm embrace.

Rose, having taken Lydia's rapt appraisal of the stranger into quick consideration and with her own curiosity nudging her, linked arms with Davy's mother. "I think we should introduce ourselves." She ushered Lydia toward where the newcomer and Hunter stood talking.

Hunter couldn't believe his eyes. He stepped back from the embrace and took in the man before him. "Hey, little brother, you're looking healthy . . ." He nodded toward the luxury car. ". . . and prosperous.

What brings you to this neck of the woods?"

Kenny grinned. "Can't I drop in on my big brother to see how he's doing?"

Ever since Kenny had graduated and moved to the West Coast, he and Hunter had only had sporadic contact. And since Kenny hadn't seen fit to *drop in* on him in over three years, Hunter couldn't swallow that explanation. "Sure, and pigs fly. Now, why are you really in West Virginia?"

Kenny laughed. "I was afraid you'd see through that. I'm actually here to look at a hotel for sale in Charleston."

"Thinking of expanding your hotel empire?" Hunter felt a surge of pride that his brother was doing so well.

Kenny's chest expanded a bit. "This will make number three. I thought I'd pick up one on the East Coast. The Green Mountain Resort. Ever hear of it?"

"Everyone around here has heard of it. Next to The Greenbrier, it's one of the biggest hotels in West Virginia. Are you —"

"Wow! Who's that?" Kenny was gaping over Hunter's shoulder.

Hunter turned. "Well, the brunette is Lydia Collins —"

"Lydia Wallace you mean? Didn't she marry George Collins right after graduation?"

"One and the same. She and George are divorced. And the redhead is Rose Hamilton, my receptionist, and she's off-limits." The words no sooner passed Hunter's lips than he wanted to snatch them back. Kenny was never gonna let this pass without explanation.

Hunter's brother didn't disappoint him. "Off-limits? Is there something I need to know?"

Immediately, a vision of the parade of girls who had passed through his handsome brother's life in high school assaulted Hunter. Thinking quickly, Hunter threw out the first thing that popped into his mind. "No. It's just that I recently lost my receptionist, and I'm not eager to have to go looking for another one just because you take a temporary liking to her."

Kenny continued to stare at the approaching women. "Actually, it was Lydia who caught my fancy. Man, she's gotten even more beautiful than when I had a crush on her in high school."

Kenny was interested in Lydia. Hunter breathed a sigh of relief, and immediately realized how foolish he was being. He was acting like the proverbial dog with the bone. He didn't want the bone, but he didn't want any other dog to have it either. Hunter, unlike the dog, had to make up his mind. He either wanted Rose for himself, or he'd have to stand back and let some other guy have her.

That thought had his stomach in knots. Rose with another man? He could more easily accept his business burning to the ground. But before he had time to think about it, the two women had reached them.

"Rose and Lydia, this is my little brother, Kenny." Without conscious thought, Hunter moved to Rose's side.

"Ken. Hello, Rose. Lydia." Kenny extended a hand to Lydia. "I haven't been Kenny in a very long time. Not since high school."

Recognition filled Lydia's expression. She let out a tiny gasp of surprise. "Oh my goodness! You're Kenny Mackenzie! You were one grade ahead of me."

"Guilty," Kenny said, flashing a charming smile at the woman whose hand he still held.

Hunter looked at Rose and saw by her expression that she felt as much like a fifth wheel as he did. "Well, we'll catch up later, *Ken.*" He took Rose's arm and steered her away from the couple.

She looked back at them over her shoulder and chuckled. "Do you think they know we left?"

By mid-afternoon, the open house was in full swing. The parking lot was a constant scene of activity as buses arrived, let off their passengers and went back for another load. Granny Jo had run out of hot dogs twice, and Hunter had to make a run to Keeler's Market for more. Lydia had snapped photos of everyone with the animals, while Ken followed her around like a faithful puppy.

Rose flopped down beside Hunter at one of the picnic tables they'd set up around Granny Jo's food tent. She sighed.

"Tired?"

She nodded and smiled. "But it's a good tired." Truth be known, her feet ached, her back hurt and a faint throbbing had begun in her left temple. But if Hunter got to keep his beloved animals, it was all worth it.

Rose watched as Lydia snapped a photo of one of the kids holding a baby lamb. "The kids are having a ball in the petting zoo."

Hunter nodded. "And we have homes set up for all of Pansy's kittens. It wasn't easy explaining to some of the kids that the kittens had to stay with their mom for a few more weeks. They wanted to scoop them up and take them home today."

"Can you blame them? Those kittens are adorable."

Suddenly, Hunter's hand closed over hers. She knew she should pull back, but reasoned that with all these people around, it would be safe to just enjoy the feel of him touching her again. Besides, she hadn't seen him smile this much in weeks.

"Thanks, Rose. You did something that I haven't been able to do. I think the townspeople will be more inclined to accept the refuge now."

"No thanks needed. It was fun and very satisfying to see that the idea worked." She squeezed his hand. "However, if you really feel like you need to thank me, you can make another one of those delicious steak dinners for me."

He grinned. "You're on."

Hunter couldn't seem to stop smiling. The open house was a success. Rose wanted to have dinner with him again. His brother had come to visit, and the people of Carson were seeing that the animals posed no threat to the community. Everything was going so well. Hunter sighed and finally relaxed.

And then all hell broke loose.

Chapter 11

From the other end of the parking lot came squeals mixed with laughter and cheering. Because a crowd had gathered, Hunter couldn't see what was causing the uproar. He grabbed Rose's hand, and they raced toward the commotion. They elbowed their way through the people and stopped dead in their tracks.

Rose couldn't believe her eyes.

George Collins raced around the trunk of a large maple tree with Rosebud hot on his heels. Davy followed right behind the twosome, frantically yelling the hog's name and screaming for her to stop.

"Rosebud, no! Bad piggy! Stop! That's my dad, and he's gonna be real mad at you. Stop, Rosebud!"

Red-faced and sweating, George ran in circles in a useless attempt to get away from the snorting baby hog. Round and round they went while the townspeople stood by, making no effort to rescue their mayor and laughing uproariously at his predicament.

At one point, Davy got a hold on Rosebud, but she slithered from his grasp and went back to her pursuit. George had never looked so disheveled. His hair stuck out in all directions. His smart, custom-tailored, navy suit, encrusted with splotches of mud and sporting a big tear in one knee, gave evidence that he had fallen several times. The red power tie that he habitually wore hung askew and the tail of his white shirt had pulled from the waistband of his slacks. His face glowed red with the exertion, and his hands were caked with dirt. His wing-tipped shoes, which were covered with mud and dust, no longer shined. In short, the neatly dressed, peacock-strutting mayor of Carson looked like the deflated loser in a barroom brawl.

Rose fought to hold back her laughter. Hunter threw her a reprimanding glare, but she could see the signs of a suppressed grin teasing at his mouth.

"She runs really fast for having an injured leg," Rose offered calmly.

"Yes, she does. I suppose we should do something," Hunter finally said, his laughter very close to the surface.

"What happens if she catches him?"

Hunter shrugged. "He'd be okay. She's not old enough to hurt him."

"Rosebud, you shouldn't be doing this," Davy was yelling, still racing after the hog, which was still hot on George's tail. The boy's face mirrored his agitated state. His cheeks glowed and his forehead glistened with beads of perspiration.

Hunter sighed. "I guess I should take pity on Davy. It's time to rescue George, even if I'd rather see him run around for another hour or so." The laughter finally broke loose. He turned his back to the crowd and got control of himself. Rose dipped her head to hide her laughter.

A roar went up from the gathered throng. Rose and Hunter jumped, and then turned to see what had caused it. To their surprise, George had managed to haul himself up onto a low-hanging branch of the spreading maple and clung to the trunk like a drowning man hanging on to a life preserver. His buttocks hung over the limb, mere inches from the hog's nose. Below him Rosebud stood guard and . . . waited.

Davy quickly scooped Rosebud up and headed for the cage from which she'd escaped. Rose followed him.

"How did she get out, Davy?"

The boy hung his head, and then lifted

his gaze to look at her. "I gave her some water, and I guess I didn't latch the cage good." His lower lip began to tremble, and then tears suddenly poured down his face. "It's all my fault. My dad's ripping mad. Doc'll prob'ly have to get rid of the animals and all 'cause of me." Sobs tore from the boy.

Rose gathered him in a hug. "It's not your fault, honey. It could have happened to anyone, even Doc or me. It was an accident."

Davy hiccupped and mumbled, "Will Doc fire me?"

Moving him so she could look him in the eyes, Rose smiled and wiped away the tears with the pad of her thumb. "Get rid of the best helper he's ever had? I don't think so. We all make mistakes, Davy. I made the mistake of letting Pansy and Thomas get together, and Pansy got pregnant because of me. Doc didn't fire me." She smoothed his cheek. "He's a good man. And he's very forgiving."

Unbidden, a thought popped into her head. Would Hunter forgive her for not telling him about the twins?

Davy, shoulders slumped in defeat, walked away and climbed into Sadie's cage, where he buried his face in the wolf's neck and sobbed some more.

Feeling helpless to comfort the boy, Rose glanced across the parking lot to where a disheveled George was shaking his finger in Hunter's face.

"This is the last straw, Mackenzie. I tried to tell you those animals were dangerous, but oh no, you wouldn't hear of it. You kept saying they weren't. Well, what do you call that creature who was trying to eat me?" George's face was crimson.

Hunter could plainly see that reasoning with the mayor was useless, but he tried anyway. "George, the hog is a baby. Even if she caught up with you the most she'd have done was rip a pant leg or something equally as unthreatening."

George stomped his foot. "Unthreatening my —" For a second or two, George sputtered trying not to say the curses that he so obviously wanted to use. Finally, he took a deep breath. "That vicious thing was out for my blood." He stepped closer to Hunter. So close that Hunter could feel his breath on his cheeks. "Mark my words, Mackenzie. I will see to it that none of these beasts threaten anyone ever again." He spun around and stalked off toward his car.

Hunter stared after him, the bottom of his

stomach rising up in dread. Something told him that what he'd found humorous moments before would ring the death knell for the refuge.

Unfortunately, the episode with George and Rosebud seemed to have put a dampener on the day, and very quickly thereafter almost everyone had returned to town, the tents had been dismantled and the animals had all been returned to their respective cages. The parking lot had lost its carnival atmosphere and looked like it normally did on any work day.

Hunter watched Lydia talking to Kenny, then climbing in her car and driving away with Davy. Kenny came toward him, his face split in a satisfied grin. "I've got a date for Saturday night."

Hunter forced a smile, then rearranged his expression into one of dead seriousness. "Do me one favor. Lydia has had enough of the downside of life for a while. Don't mess with her heart. Don't hurt her."

Isn't that exactly what you're doing to Rose? Perhaps you should take your own advice.

Ignoring the niggling little voice of his conscience, Hunter waited for Kenny's reply.

His brother's expression also grew serious. "Lydia was never a one-night-stand kind of woman in high school and I can't see that that has changed at all. And to put your mind at ease, I would never hurt her or her son by playing fast and loose with her heart. Right now, it's just two friends having dinner to talk about old times."

Hunter hesitated, and then nodded. "Good. Now, let's go pop a couple of beers, get the grill started while we catch up, and then we'll throw on some steaks."

As they walked, they met Rose heading for her apartment. Hunter stopped her. "We're gonna throw some steaks on. Want to collect on that dinner I owe you?"

She paused before answering. "Wouldn't I be intruding? Don't you two want some time alone?"

Kenny threw Rose one his charmer smiles. "A beautiful woman is never an intrusion."

Hunter groaned and fought down the green monster that raised its head every time another man came close to Rose. Kenny hadn't changed one bit — ever the lady's man. When he was in high school, Hunter remembered a never-ending parade of different girls that passed through their house every weekend.

Hunter glared at his brother. "No intrusion. We'll see you on the patio as soon as you're ready."

Rose smiled up at the younger Mackenzie. "Okay. I'll make a salad and be down in an hour or so." She glanced at Hunter and hurried off.

When she was safely out of earshot, Hunter turned to Kenny. "Off-limits. Remember that."

Hunter popped the top on his beer and settled back in the chaise lounge. The steaks were soaking in Hunter's special marinade; flames shot off the charcoal in the grill and would take a while to burn off to red coals for cooking. He and Kenny had plenty of time to kick back and get reacquainted.

"So, Little Bro, you're buying another hotel?" Kenny nodded. "Gonna become another Donald Trump."

Kenny laughed. "Hardly. I'm just addicted to buying them and either pulling them out of the financial cellar or making them better than when I got them."

Hunter sipped his beer and relished the cold liquid sliding down his throat. "So which is the Green Mountain Resort? A financial rescue or a building block?" He set his can on the table between them.

"The latter. Financially, it's doing really well, but the owner's looking to retire. I stopped there on my way up here, and I see a lot of potential for add-ons and improvements that should boost the revenue through the roof."

For a moment, Hunter stared at his little brother, marveling at the successful life he'd built for himself. "You've come a long way. I'm proud of you, Ken."

Ken continued to look out toward Hawks Mountain where the peaks were outlined by the setting sun. "I couldn't have done it without you and your sacrifices. I never said *thank you* for all you did back then. Janice and I wouldn't be where we are today without your help and guidance. You gave up so much for us, and don't for a minute think we don't know it or appreciate it."

Neither brother looked at the other. A lump formed in Hunter's throat, preventing him from saying anything. His siblings had never expressed their appreciation before for what he'd done back then, for all he'd given up so they could have careers, and it moved him beyond words.

"You'll never know what an impact you had on our lives, Hunter, the example you set by stepping in and taking over for Mom and Dad. You were really just past being a kid yourself, but you grew up very fast. Not many people could or would have done what you did, gave up what you did." He finally looked at Hunter. "Thank you for being my brother, my friend and my parent and being so good at all three."

Hunter could only nod and smile. Words just would not pass the emotions shutting off his throat.

Ken scrubbed his thumb across the sweat on his beer can while they both worked their way through the emotions and the discomfort of expressing feelings that they'd never talked about before.

"So, tell me about this lady who's off-limits. Exactly what's happening between you two?" His voice held the telltale scratchiness of suppressed emotion.

Ken's question threw Hunter into a mental panic. He hadn't come to terms with himself concerning his feelings for Rose. How could he answer his brother's question without stepping into a swamp that could suck him under?

"She's my receptionist. That's all." Hunter got up and went to the grill, but Ken followed.

A robust laugh burst from Ken. "And pigs fly, too."

Stirring the coals, Hunter sought another topic of conversation. "How long will you be around here?" But his tenacious brother wasn't that easily sidetracked.

"Don't try changing the subject. I saw the way you looked at her and she looked at you. That was love, brother dear, pure, unadulterated love if I ever saw it." He leaned against the tree a few feet away and crossed his arms. "So what do you plan on doing about it?"

"Doing?"

"Yes, as in taking her out, proposing —"

"Whoa!" Hunter held up a hand. "You're moving kinda fast. We've never been out on a date, and you're talking marriage proposals."

"Well, isn't it about time you did go on a date then?"

"No. That leads to too many other things, one of which can be marriage, and I'm not marriage material."

Ken's arms dropped to his sides, and his mouth fell open. "Are you kidding me? You'd make a perfect dad to some kid and a wonderful husband. Where did you ever get the idea that you wouldn't?"

How could Hunter tell Ken, after what he'd just said about how appreciative they were for all he'd done, that Ken and Janice and all the effort and sacrifice that had gone into playing surrogate parent to them had soured him on having a family of his own to

195

be responsible for? If he wasn't careful, he could alienate his brother and perhaps his sister.

"Family life is just not for me, so can we just drop it, Ken?"

"Drop what?" Rose placed a bowl full of salad fixings on the patio table, along with two bottles of salad dressing. Then she looked from one man to the other.

Neither of them had heard Rose approach. Hunter's heart dropped to his stomach. How much of the conversation had she overheard?

CHAPTER 12

"Well?" Rose repeated. "Drop what?"

Thinking quickly, Hunter shook his head and blurted, "Nothing. Ken and I were just reminiscing, and it was getting a bit emotional."

"Yeah, emotional," Ken added with a sly wink at Hunter.

Ken gripped Rose's arm and guided her to a chaise lounge a few feet from the grill. He dropped onto the other one, leaned back, crossed his legs at the ankles and folded his hands over his stomach. "So, Rose, tell me how you met my handsome older brother." He wiggled his eyebrows and grinned like a Cheshire cat.

Hunter glared at his brother and mouthed, *Let it go.* Ken ignored him.

"We met when I applied for the job as his receptionist." Rose looked questioning from one brother to the other. Something was going on, but she had no idea what. And somehow, she felt it concerned her. Given the underlying innuendos in Ken's question, Rose decided it would be safer to avoid the subject of her and Hunter.

Instead, she turned to Hunter. "So what did our illustrious mayor have to say after Rosebud gave him a run for his money?"

Hunter's expression seemed to crumble, and she immediately regretted bringing up the subject of George Collins.

"Nothing good, I'm afraid."

Ken sat straighter. "What's that mean?"

Hunter flipped over the steaks and for a long moment, the sounds of sizzling meat filled the pregnant silence. Then he dropped the tongs on the shelf at the side of the grill and turned to them.

"He's threatening to shut me down. Get rid of all the wild animals."

"Is that all? How many times have we fielded that threat?" Rose said, trying to ease the lines of tension around Hunter's mouth with flippancy.

A forced smile curved Hunter's lips. "Too many to count." Just as quickly, all humor vanished from his expression and the tension returned. "I always viewed them as idle threats. A cause for him to champion. Then lately, a way to keep Davy away from here. The problem is, he's never been attacked

198

by one of the animals before, and this time I think he's going to carry through. This time he has facts to back his claims, and the entire town to bear witness that our animals are dangerous."

Rose jumped to her feet. Fear, concern, anger and a million other emotions coursed through her. "Attacked? He's calling what happened with Rosebud an attack? Good grief, she's a baby."

" 'Fraid so." Hunter went back to tending the steaks, defeat apparent in the slump of his shoulders.

"Why would he do such a thing?" Ken asked.

"Because he has some wild idea that a baby lion that's barely old enough to eat on its own is going to attack him while he sleeps." She lowered her voice. "We should be so lucky."

Ken's eyes open wide. "What? That's crazy. I didn't see one animal today that looked dangerous to me. You can't let him do this, Hunter."

Hunter shrugged and said nothing.

He's giving up. He's going to let that blow-hard win.

Anger at Hunter's defeatist attitude and George's ridiculous claims fused inside Rose. The survival skills that had been her salvation in all the foster homes she'd lived in flooded her. "We won't let him. I won't. These people know Rosebud is just a baby. He won't be able to sway the town council with such flimsy evidence. Besides, they all saw it for themselves and everyone was laughing. If they'd felt he was in danger, someone other than a ten-year-old boy, who was probably more concerned about the pig than the man, would have come to his rescue." She moved to Hunter's side and laid her hand on his arm. "You can't give up. These animals need you . . . you need them."

"She's right, you know," Ken added. "You're stronger than that. The Hunter I grew up with would not give in to this jerk."

Hunter looked at them, his face drawn and troubled. "I may not have a choice."

By the time the steaks and salad had been eaten, the mood had lightened some. Hunter didn't look as downtrodden as he had and was even able to smile from time to time at Ken's memories of a mischievous childhood. Rose sipped on a bottle of spring water, while the men each indulged in another beer. A balmy breeze blew through the valley making the trees sway, and the sky had come alive with twinkling stars which were mirrored in the abundance of fireflies glittering in the trees and bushes like Christmas twinkle lights.

Everything seemed so very peaceful, but close to the surface of her thoughts and, without a doubt, Hunter's, was the very real possibility that George would make good his threat to close the refuge. By the time Ken excused himself and sauntered off to bed, the subject had ripened to be raised again.

"So, what do we do now?" The defeat in Hunter's voice made Rose's heart twist in her chest.

"We fight."

He rose and walked to the edge of the lawn. "I'm not sure I have any fight left in me."

Rose followed him. She turned him toward her and cupped his face in her palms. "Then use my fight. You can't give in to him." Then she wrapped her arms around him. "I won't let you," she whispered in his ear. "We're in this together."

His arms came around her and pulled her close. "Whatever I did that made the Fates decide that I deserved you, I'm everlastingly grateful. If only life could be as peaceful as it is at this moment . . . forever."

The wistfulness in his voice brought burning tears to Rose's eyes. There could never be a forever for them, not as long as Hunter didn't want the responsibility of a family. She sniffled.

"Rose? Are you crying?" Hunter pushed her back and looked at her face. "What is it? Is it the problem with the animals?"

Darn! She hadn't wanted him to see her tears. She wiped at them. "No."

"What then? Tell me." He led her back to the chaise lounge, guided her down in the seat, and then sat beside her, holding her hand.

Her mind whirled. She couldn't very well tell him that she was crying because they could never have a relationship, so she grabbed at the first thing that entered her mind. "Davy is going to be crushed. If they take the other animals, they most certainly will take Sadie, too."

Hunter nodded, but said nothing. Neither did she. What was there to say? His shoulders seemed to slump a bit more.

His defeat seeped into her. She could feel it sucking her down into a pit of hopeless depression. Her determination had started to give way to accepting their downfall, but she couldn't allow that and fought her way back up to the top. The rock-hard, determined Rose emerged, angry about George's shortsightedness and angry with Hunter for even thinking in terms of defeat before it happened.

The Rose that had survived her mother's abandonment, foster homes, the death of her best friend and the knowledge that she would soon be the single mother of twins surfaced. If they stopped feeling sorry for themselves and put their heads together, they could beat George. She was sure of it.

Her back stiffened. She wiped at her cheeks. "Look at us. Are we two of the saddest sacks you've ever seen? What we need to be doing is getting together a plan to stop George, not sitting here bemoaning what *could* happen. We can do it if we do it together."

Hunter smiled for perhaps the first time since Ken went to bed. "Together." Then he kissed her cheek. "Is there anything that makes you cry uncle, Rose Hamilton?"

Yes, she thought. *How to convince you that a family is not a burden but a joy.*

The following morning, much to Rose's surprise, Granny Jo appeared in the office. She set a wicker basket of blueberry muffins on the counter.

"Granny Jo, Jake doesn't have an appointment, so what brings you here?"

"I just felt like some girl talk, and since my Becky's off at a meeting in Charleston with the Social Service people, and I have all these hot muffins to share with someone, I thought of you." She patted the handle of the basket. "I hope you've got some coffee made to go with these muffins. I've only had one cup, and it takes at least three to get my motor running properly." She grinned devilishly.

Rose jumped to her feet, her mouth already salivating from the smell of the muffins. "Hunter just drank the last of it before he left to make some house calls, but if you'll have a seat, I'll have some ready in just a shake." She hurried into the back room and made a fresh pot of decaf coffee, then returned to the reception area while it brewed. She took a seat in one of the molded plastic chairs. "It shouldn't take long. Hope you don't mind decaf."

"Nope. Decaf's fine. I suppose it's better for a pregnant lady to drink decaf. In my day, it didn't much matter what you drank."

Rose barely heard any of the words that followed *pregnant lady*. "How . . ."

Granny laid her hand on Rose's. "Did you really think I came here to eat muffins and drink coffee with you? Something told me yesterday that there's a burden praying on your mind, and since you don't know anyone in town, I thought you could use a friendly ear to lighten the load." She sat back.

"But how did you know I'm pregnant?"

"Child, when you get to be my age, you can recognize the signs a mile off. Besides," she waved a finger at Rose's tummy, "you're getting a bit . . . thick around the middle."

Rose laid her hand on her stomach. She knew she'd put on a few pounds, but she really hadn't thought she'd gained enough weight to show.

"Now, don't you start fretting that Hunter will find out. Men just don't notice things like that. Besides, it doesn't show all that much."

This was uncanny. "How did you know that I haven't told Hunter?"

Granny Jo laughed. "I don't have the sight, if that's what you're thinking. That was just a real good guess." She paused for a moment. "You're in love with him, aren't you?"

Wow! This lady was way too observant for Rose's peace of mind. "I'm not —"

Before Rose could finish her denial, Granny waved her hand. "Save your breath. Any blind man can see the way you look at him, like he's the one who hung the moon."

Then she frowned. "So why haven't you told him about the baby?"

"Babies. I'm carrying twins." Leaning back in the chair, Rose sighed. "It's complicated."

"Twins, huh? A double blessing." Patting her hand, Granny smiled knowingly. "Well, complicated is a specialty of mine. You go get us some coffee, and then we'll talk. Maybe I can help you untangle this mess."

Feeling a little apprehensive about sharing her secret with anyone, Rose got the coffee and returned to the reception area a few moments later. She set the tray holding the coffee carafe, two mugs, a sugar bowl, and a pitcher of cream on the table between them and poured the coffee, then leaned back and began talking.

Rose hadn't meant to tell Granny everything, but the whole story had suddenly come pouring out to this sweet lady with the compassionate face and knowing eyes. By the time they'd consumed half the basket of muffins and several cups of coffee, Granny Jo knew it all: Rose's childhood betrayal by her mother and subsequent life in foster homes, her friendship with Beth, her agreement to carry the baby for Beth, Beth's death and finally, what Hunter had confided in her about not wanting the responsibility of a family. The one thing she didn't share was her doubts about her qualifications for motherhood.

To Rose's surprise, Granny Jo laughed when she told her the last part about Hunter not wanting responsibility. "Men! They can't see the path ahead of them because they're too busy stepping over the rocks in their way." Then she sobered. "As for not wanting responsibility . . . why, my Lord, child, the man must be blind. He's got more responsibility right here taking care of these animals than any father I know."

Rose refilled their cups. "But animals don't go to college or get into trouble."

"But they're as much like kids as the real thing. Don't know of any that go to college, but they need tending every day, feeding, watering, medical attention, loving. And they do get into trouble every now and again." Granny grinned and winked at her.

Setting the coffee carafe aside, Rose hid her smile. She knew Granny Jo was thinking about Rosebud chasing George.

"Granny, what can we do about George?"

The older woman's eyebrows rose in unison. "Changing the subject?"

Her cheeks heated. Rose nodded.

The older woman sipped her coffee, and

then set the cup on the table and picked up a muffin. "Well, that's been a problem we in Carson have been asking ever since we elected him to office. Mind you, I didn't vote for him. I knew right off he was a horse's backside, but he managed to horn-swoggle the rest of the folks or at least enough for him to win. Unfortunately, we're stuck with him until elections come around in a few months." She stripped the muffin's paper cup off and set it aside, took a bite and chewed thoughtfully then swallowed. "But I don't suppose that's what you meant."

"No, I was referring to him trying to close down the animal refuge."

"Honey, he has to get that notion past the town council first."

Rose wished she had as much faith in the town as Granny did. "Even after what happened yesterday?"

Granny stood and retrieved the empty basket. "Especially after yesterday. Don't sell the people of Carson short. They'll do the right thing." She headed for the door. "Now, I've taken enough of your time. But just remember that problems very often have a way of sorting themselves out without our interference. Then there's some," she said, pointing to Rose's tummy, "that needs a nudge in the right direction." She cupped Rose's cheek. "Tell him, child. You may be surprised at his reaction."

Rose stood in the doorway and watched Granny drive away. Was she right? Should she just tell Hunter about the twins and hope for the best? Whatever she decided, she was not about to burden him with another problem until the George thing was solved. Hopefully, that would be sooner rather than later.

Several days later, the sound of several trucks coming up the driveway startled Rose.

CHAPTER 13

At the unusual sound of truck motors in the parking lot, Hunter came out of the back room.

"Do we have a feed delivery due?" He passed a puzzled-looking Rose on his way to the front door.

She followed quickly behind him. "No. We just got one a few days ago."

Just outside the front door, Hunter came up so short that he felt Rose stop her forward motion by bracing her hands against his back. He stared at the sight in the parking lot. "What the —"

Two trucks, parked one behind the other, had just come to a halt in front of the wild animal rehab building. One, a small pickup with a cap on the back, had a large green circle with the picture of a wolf in the center painted on the driver's door. Encircling the wolf's head were the words: *West Virginia Wolf Preservation Project.* The other, a much larger pickup pulling a closed-in box trailer had a sign on it reading *Monongahela Wildlife Refuge*.

At that moment, Sheriff Ainsley pulled up in his patrol car, got out and spoke to the two men, then pointed toward the building that housed the wild animals. As Hunter watched the men head for the wild animal rehab building, a hard knot of dread began to form in his gut.

Ainsley followed their progress for a moment, then turned and strode purposefully toward Hunter and Rose. He carried a white sheet of paper. Hunter's heart sunk. He had an awful feeling he knew exactly what that paper meant.

Ainsley removed his hat and nodded a silent greeting.

"Sheriff, what's going on?" A totally unnecessary question. In his heart, Hunter already knew the answer. George had gotten to the town council, and Hunter was about to reap the whirlwind of the open house fiasco.

'Doc, I'm as sorry as I can be about this . . .." He held out the paper.

Hunter stared down at it, unable to reach for it. He knew when he did that his fears would be proven right.

"It's a court order to remove the wild

animals, Doc." Ainsley lowered his voice and leaned closer to Hunter. "I hear that the mayor has been working on the town council for the last few days and convinced them that the animals had to go. If you ask me, it should be the other way around. Lord only knows how he did it, seeing as how they all had such a good time at your open house and . . ." The words trailed off, and Ainsley looked a bit embarrassed as though he suddenly realized he'd been babbling to fill the awkward silence.

Rose took the paper and read it. Her face confirmed Hunter's worst fears. "He can't do this . . . can he?"

" 'Fraid so, ma'am. He's the mayor and . . . Well, the judge signed off on it, and I got no choice but to serve the doc here and make sure he complies."

Rose grabbed Hunter's arm. "We can take him to court and get it reversed."

Hunter turned to look into her tear-filled eyes. Rose never ceased to amaze him with her unshakable belief that they could beat George at his own game. Unfortunately, that was looking less and less likely. This time the mayor had the law on his side, and Hunter's hands were tied. "I wish I could, but I can't afford the kind of money it would take to get a lawyer and fight this,

Rose. I'm afraid we have no choice but to let them take the animals."

Before he could say more, a man emerged from the animal rehab building and called to them. "Hey, there's a kid in the cage with the wolf, and he won't let me take her. Can somebody reason with him?"

Together, Hunter and Rose whispered, "Davy!" Then they ran toward the building.

The man from the wolf preservation project followed them inside. "I explained why I was here to the kid, but when I try to remove the wolf, he yells, and then she bares her teeth."

"Don't let them take Sadie, Doc, please!" Davy's tear-stained face peered at Hunter over Sadie's shaggy back, his arms wrapped firmly around the animal's neck. The wolf's yellow-eyed gaze never left the people standing around her cage.

"Davy trusts me. Let me talk to him."

Hunter grasped her arm. She smiled at him. "I have to try." He studied her for a moment, then nodded and let her go.

Rose moved closer to the cage. Sadie's top lip curled up, and she emitted a deep-throated snarl. Rose paused and waited.

"It's okay, Sadie. It's Miss Rose. She's our friend." The wolf quieted, but kept her large, gray body stationed solidly between anyone outside the cage and Davy. A pair of wary eyes rested on Rose.

Rose squatted near the cage. "Davy, this man is from the wolf preservation project. He's not going to hurt Sadie. He just wants to take her to live with the other wild animals, where she'll be able to be with her own kind."

"No." Davy tightened his hold on the wolf's neck. "She's not wild. If she was, I couldn't be in her cage with her. And she doesn't need to go there. She likes it here with me and you and the doc."

Realizing this was going to take a while, Rose sat cross-legged on the floor beside the cage. She leaned forward. Sadie emitted another throaty growl.

"Shhh," Davy said, running his hand over the wolf's flank. "It's okay."

Rose's heart went out to the boy. Sadie had become like his pet dog, and separating him from her would devastate him. Rose blinked away the tears threatening to fall and then swallowed back the emotional lump gathering in her throat.

"Davy, they'll take really good care of Sadie. She'll be able to find a boy wolf, and they'll make babies together and have a real family."

"No, I'm her family."

Rose shook her head. This was tearing at her insides. "No, not really. Only other wolves can be Sadie's real family. You're her friend. Her very best friend, but she needs other wolves to have a real family."

"Rose," Hunter called across the room. "It's time."

Rose waved him off with a swipe of her hand.

"Okay. Here's the thing, Davy." She paused, hating to use this argument, but seeing no other way to persuade him to let the man take Sadie. "A judge says that Doc has to let them take all the wild animals. If he doesn't . . . if you don't let them take Sadie, Doc will go to jail. You don't want him to be locked up in a cage, do you?"

Davy shook his head. Fresh tears cascaded down his cheeks. "No. But I don't want them to take Sadie either."

"I know, sweetheart, but you're gonna have to. And besides, if you let Sadie go with this man, she'll be able to run through the forests instead of being locked up in this cage all the time. It's not fair to her to keep her here when she could be free, is it?"

Davy said nothing, but she could see, by the deep frown lines in his forehead, that he was considering what she'd said.

She wanted to cry or scream or something.

Anything that would stop this and make it all go away — make Davy smile again and take the slump from Hunter's shoulders.

God, this is just so wrong. What in Heaven's name is George thinking by sending these men here? Doesn't he care about his son at all? Davy loves that animal so very much, and it's obvious that the wolf loves him. Separating them is just beyond unfair. It borders on criminal.

Finally, the boy spoke, his tone low and accusing. "My dad did this, didn't he? Just 'cause Rosebud chased him around the yard?" His voice, though still choked with tears, had grown angry.

Rose didn't answer. How could she? Whatever else George was, he was still Davy's father. She didn't have to answer. Davy wasn't stupid. He knew who to blame.

"I hate him!" Davy screamed. "I hate him!"

Even the wolf sensed something was terribly wrong. Following Davy's outburst, Sadie threw back her head and howled the most mournful howl Rose had ever heard from her. The sound washed right through her, making her shiver with the intensity of sadness it held.

Rose didn't try to argue with Davy. At this very moment, he probably did hate his father. Nothing would make him feel differently. She sighed. What more could she say to persuade him to let Sadie go? She'd used up all her arguments.

Hunter had come to stand beside Rose. "Davy, bring Sadie out of the cage," he said, his tone gentle, but firm. "She has to go now."

The boy glanced at Hunter. "But, Doc —"

"Now, Davy. Please. For me."

Reading his resignation in the sudden slump of the boy's slim shoulders and the anguish in his face, Rose fought back her tears. "Davy, you need to do as Doc says."

After wiping his nose on the sleeve of his shirt, Davy sniffed and stood. "Can I take her to the truck?"

Rose looked over her shoulder at the man from the preserve. "Can he?"

The man stared at the boy and the wolf. "Take this to tie around her neck." He held out a rope with a loop in the end.

Rose smiled and shook her head. "He doesn't need a rope."

Still the man hesitated to give his permission. "You sure?"

"As sure as I am that the sun will come up tomorrow."

He hesitated for a moment longer, and then nodded his okay.

She turned back to Davy. "Yes, you can take her."

The boy stood and threw his arm over Sadie's back. "Come on girl." Together they left the cage.

Everyone stood back while Davy led the big wolf from the cage, his hand resting on the scruff of her neck. Davy looked too small and too skinny to have such control over a full-grown timber wolf, but Sadie walked docilely beside him like a well-trained dog.

The man from the preservation project watched openmouthed and shook his head. "I don't believe this."

Rose had a flashback to the first time she saw Davy in the cage with Sadie, and the wolf had gently taken food from Davy's mouth. She smiled recalling her own disbelief. "Believe it. He's a miniature Dr. Dolittle."

Hunter's arm slid around her shoulders. "He's *our* Dr. Dolittle." A wistful sadness colored his voice as he watched the wolf and boy walk out of the building.

Everyone followed the pair outside and across the parking lot to the truck.

"Up, Sadie," Davy told her. The wolf jumped agilely from the ground to the bed of the truck and walked inside the cage. She lay down and faced Davy. He threw his arms around her and hugged her. "I love you, Sadie. Don't forget me. I'll never forget you." Then he buried his face in the wolf's fur and sobbed.

A few minutes later, the man gently laid his hand on Davy's shoulder. "We have to go now, son."

Rose wiped away the tears that, despite her best efforts to stop them, had finally escaped and were now streaming freely down her face. She walked to the boy and pulled him away from the truck. The man closed the cage door and then the door to the truck's cap. He turned back to Davy. "We'll take really good care of her, son. She'll have a whole forest to run in and lots of other wolves to keep her company." Then, he climbed into the driver's seat.

Moments later the truck's motor roared to life. The sheriff's car followed by the two trucks, one holding Sadie and the other holding the remainder of the wild animals, moved slowly down the driveway.

Davy threw himself into Rose's arms. She cradled him close, smoothing his hair and trying to sooth his broken heart. The mournful howl of the wolf broke the silence of the late afternoon. There would be no assuaging either of them for a long time.

■ ■ ■ ■

Hunter balanced the cold can of beer on his stomach, stretched his legs out on the chaise lounge and stared absently into the distance at the silhouette of Hawks Mountain against the star-studded summer sky. His stomach growled for lack of supper, but he'd had no appetite, and since Ken had gone off to have dinner with Lydia, there hadn't been any reason to pretend.

Truthfully, his thoughts were far from food. He kept hearing Davy's cries and Sadie's howls and wondering what he could have done to stop it. But nothing came to mind. How could he fight a court order?

It seemed impossible that in the last twenty-four hours he'd lost so much of his life. So much that mattered to him. So much —

But had he? Yes, he'd lost the wild animals, and they had definitely mattered. But he still had his veterinarian practice, his home and . . . and Rose. Thoughts of Rose brought with them an urgent need to see her, to talk about the day's events. To share his day with someone who cared.

But would she want to see him? Was she in need of someone to talk to, also? There was only one way to find out.

Resolutely, he set the beer can on the table beside the chaise, stood, took a deep breath and then hurried toward Rose's apartment. As he made his way around the building to her door, he told himself this visit was purely because he needed company, some-one to talk to, a friendly, sympathetic ear and nothing more.

But when he got to her door and raised his hand to knock, he hesitated. The realiza-tion slammed into him that he didn't just need *someone* to talk to. He needed Rose. And that scared him to his toes. Hunter Mackenzie. The man who didn't want a family, didn't want the responsibility that went with it, needed someone else.

He dropped his hand and stared at the wooden blockade between him and a woman who had somehow managed to become essential to his peace of mind. Dare he risk going in there?

CHAPTER 14

Rose had been trying unsuccessfully to block out the events of the day by attempting to read a book when a knock sounded on her door. She glanced at the clock. Ten forty-eight. Who could possibly be at her door at this hour? Laying the book aside, she hurried to the head of the stairs.

"Who is it?"

"Hunter."

For a moment, surprise rendered her silent. Hunter hadn't been here since the night they'd had dinner and made — No, she refused to go there. Until this moment, she'd been able to shove that to the back of her mind, and was almost able to pretend it never happened. And with him standing outside her door asking for admittance, it was no time for her to walk down memory lane.

"Rose?"

She roused herself from her thoughts.

"Ah, yes. I'm sorry. Come in."

The door swung open and in the dim stair light she could see his disheveled state. His brown hair looked as if he'd been combing it with his fingers, and his shirt hung half out of the waistband of his trousers. Certainly not the well-groomed man she was used to seeing every day. As he got closer and stepped into the lamplight, worry lines that had seemingly appeared in the last few hours marked his face. Shadows of the day's disappointments lingered in his eyes.

Rose understood his emotional state. Deep inside her matching shadows cloaked her heart. Had they done all they could to stop George? Could they have somehow prevented Davy from losing Sadie? The questions had tormented her for hours, and she was sure Hunter as well. Nevertheless, seeing him like this tore her apart. How she wished she could do something, anything to lessen his burden.

As he topped the stairs, she laid her hand on his arm. "Are you okay?" Stupid question. Of course he wasn't okay.

"Yes." Then he smiled wanly. "Actually, no, I'm not. I needed a friendly face and someone to talk to."

She grabbed at the first thought that crossed her mind. With all that had gone on today, she hadn't eaten, and her guess was Hunter hadn't either. "Have you eaten?"

He shook his head.

"Neither have I. Have a seat, and I'll fix us a sandwich." She hurried off to the kitchen area and quickly threw together a couple of ham sandwiches and opened two cans of soda. She set them on a tray and then carried it back to the living room and set the tray on the coffee table in front of him.

Hunter stared at the food as if it were poison, but picked it up and took a bite, and then replaced it on the plate. "Nothing against your sandwich, but I'm not really very hungry."

Truth be told, she didn't much want the sandwich either. The food would have never passed the lump that had lodged in her throat ever since the trucks had driven off with all the animals, and she'd called Lydia to pick up Davy.

Rose put Davy in Lydia's car, and with Davy's cries for his beloved Sadie still echoing in her head, Rose had excused herself and hurried to her apartment where she'd finally allowed her unrestrained tears to fall. And now, though as equally depressed as Hunter, she forced herself to put on a brave front for him.

For a long time, she and Hunter just sat there in a thickening stillness, each engulfed in their own thoughts, neither wanting to put them into words.

Finally, Rose could stand the silence no longer. "Where's Ken tonight?"

Pulled from his thoughts, Hunter stirred and looked blankly at her for a second. Then he blinked, as if her words had just registered in his brain. "Uh . . . he took Lydia to dinner. They went into Charleston somewhere, I think."

"What about Davy?" The thought of the poor child having to spend any time with George after he'd ripped the boy's heart out, brought Rose to high alert. "They didn't leave him with his father did they?"

"No. Originally, Ken had planned on just him and Lydia going out. But after what happened today, he insisted they take Davy along." Hunter's lips curved into a weary smile. "I think my brother likes the boy as much as he likes his mom."

Silence fell again.

Finally, Rose broached the subject they'd both been avoiding. "What do you plan to do to stop George?"

Hunter stood and walked to the window overlooking the entire compound. "I don't want to talk about it."

She stood and went to his side. "You said you came up here because you needed someone to talk to. If it's not to talk, then why did you come here? What do you want, Hunter?"

Hunter turned slowly from the window. He looked into her beautiful eyes. The answer to her question hit him with all the force of a semi barreling brakeless down Hawks Mountain. He wanted *her,* and not just physically and not just now. He wanted her tomorrow, next week, next month, next year — forever — beside him to share his life, the ups and downs, the triumphs and the failures, the good and the bad.

"This is what I want." He pulled her to him and kissed her quite thoroughly. Using the kiss, he tried to convey to her all that she meant to him, all the feelings he'd been holding back because he was still too hesitant to put them into words.

At first, Rose stood stiffly within his embrace. Then slowly she melted into him and clung like a morning glory to a trellis.

Just as suddenly, she pulled back.

Resting her forehead against his, she struggled for breath. "We have . . . to talk. I have to tell you about —"

Hunter shook his head and placed a finger over her lips. "Not . . . now."

"But —"

"We'll talk . . . later." His breath too was coming in short, labored gasps, and his heavily beating heart felt like it would burst from his chest. "Later," he whispered. Then he cupped her face in his hands and covered her mouth with his again.

He felt Rose hesitated for a fraction of a second, then her arms encircled his neck and her body leaned into his. He deepened the kiss, glorying in her eager response.

Holding Rose close and feeling the solidity of her against him gave birth to more than primal male urges in Hunter. It conjured up soul-soothing peace and a contentment he never seemed able to achieve when she wasn't near. The problems facing him with George and the anguished cries of a little boy who had just had his best friend ripped away faded, drowned out by the thunder of his heart and his need for the woman in his arms.

The rising sun painted golden patterns across the quilt on Rose's bed. Beside her, Hunter snored softly. The afterglow of their magical night of lovemaking still encased her in a warm cocoon.

He'd held her all night as if even in sleep he couldn't let her go. With her head on his solid shoulder and his body close to hers, she felt safe and secure for the first time in her life — like she belonged. She snuggled closer.

Rose truly loved this man and after last night, she was beginning to believe he loved her. But would it be enough? Could love overcome his resistance to having a family, especially one that came ready-made?

She rolled to her back, dislodging his arm. He moaned softly and threw it back over her middle. What she would give to stop time and spend the rest of her days right here, just like this. Oddly, the other two human beings she was responsible for were the very barriers standing between her and finding happiness with Hunter.

She slid her hand over her tummy, which had started to show a bit more in the last few weeks. Not enough to raise questions from anyone but Granny Jo's sharp eyes, but enough to warn Rose that her secret wouldn't be a secret for much longer.

"Morning." Hunter's sleepy voice came from beside her.

Propping herself up on her elbow, she smiled down at him. "Morning."

He pushed himself up and kissed her. "What time is it?"

Over his shoulder, the digital clock's red

numbers flashed eight twenty-two. "Almost eight thirty. Good thing it's Sunday, and the office is closed today."

Hunter chuckled low in his throat. The sound sent shivers up Rose's spine. Hunter pushed himself up, repositioned the pillow behind his back and leaned against the headboard. Then he gathered Rose to his chest. "Since we don't have to open the office, that gives us time to —"

Rose's body began to respond to his nearness. Knowing what he was about to suggest and fighting everything in her to keep from giving in to the need growing inside her, she levered herself away. It was time to clear the air between them. Moving to the foot of the bed, she grabbed a pillow, pulled the quilt up to her armpits and leaned against the footboard facing him. Seeing him sitting there with the sheet low across his stomach was hard enough. Lying beside him would be torture.

"We need to talk."

He frowned. "Sounds serious. What's up?"

She swallowed hard and averted her gaze, then looked back at him. "I've been keeping something from you."

"You're married."

She shook her head.

"You're quitting."

"Good heavens, no. I love my job, probably more than I've ever liked any job I've ever had."

He grinned. "I'm glad to hear you say that. Because I love having you working for me." He winked at her and then swung his legs over the side of the bed and reached for his clothes. He pulled on his shorts, then his jeans and stood. "However, I'm afraid you're either going to have to tell me what you've been hiding or give me some hints. I've run out of guesses."

Rose pulled her legs up to her chest and clasped her arms around her knees. Taking a deep breath, she said it before she could chicken out. "I'm pregnant. With twins."

Hunter stopped in the process of buttoning his shirt. "What? But we only . . ."

Rose suddenly realized what he was thinking. "No. No. It's not yours." Trying very hard not to make judgments about the stricken look on his face, she hurried on. "I was . . . am a surrogate for Beth." Quickly, she told him about Beth's inability to conceive, and her decision to carry the babies for her friend.

When she'd told him everything, she waited for his reaction. But there was none. Through it all, Hunter had never said a word, nor had he moved. And now, he stood as still as if frozen in time.

Fear curled its cold hand around her heart.

For what seemed like an eternity, he continued to stare at her, his face unreadable. Then he snatched up his shoes and headed out of the room.

Just before he disappeared out the door, he glanced back at her. "I'm sorry. I can't do it."

CHAPTER 15

When Hunter stumbled through his front door and collapsed on the couch, he was still reeling from Rose's totally unexpected announcement.

Pregnant? With twins?

Why hadn't he noticed? Surely her body had changed from the first day he'd met her and given away some clue that she was pregnant. That wasn't something a woman could hide for long.

But to him she looked just as gorgeous as she had the day she'd walked into his office looking for a job. Then he recalled that day and how Rose had gagged, and he'd joked to himself that he wasn't that bad looking. Looking back on it now, little things he'd passed off began coming back and making sense. The gagging had been what doctors oddly refer to as morning sickness, even though it can last all day. And she never drank alcohol or regular coffee, both no-

no's for a mother-to-be.

In his defense, however, none of that had really been enough to suggest pregnancy. She could have had a stomach virus that first day. As for the rest, in this age of vegetarians and elevated nutrition consciousness, it wasn't all that unusual for people not to drink alcohol or to prefer decaf coffee, especially in the evening.

Once he got past mentally chastising himself for not noticing her condition, the full impact of it set in.

He loved Rose, but he didn't want the added responsibility of two little lives to care for. He'd been there and he recalled all too vividly the restricted lifestyle he'd been forced into.

How had this happened? He'd been so careful to steer wide of relationships that could develop into more and that might include the responsibility of a family. Then he fell head over heels for a woman who came with a ready-made family. Twins, no less!

He shook his head. Between George and his antics and this new revelation from Rose, Hunter's stress level had just jumped off the charts.

Rubbing his throbbing temples, he headed for his bedroom with the hope that a shower would help him sort everything out. Or, at the very least, help him find some answers.

When he emerged from the shower twenty minutes later, his mind was still reeling. He got dressed and thanked heavens that he didn't have to go into the office and face Rose today. Grabbing his keys, he left the house, climbed in his truck and drove away with no idea of his destination except that it was away from here, away from Rose.

Rose steered her cantankerous car up Lower Mountain Road and across the bridge spanning Bender's Creek on a steady course toward Granny Jo Hawks' house. After Hunter had walked out, she had spent almost an hour feeling sorry for herself and soaking several dozen tissues with useless tears. When she'd heard his truck drive out of the compound, she'd cried even harder.

By the time she got herself under control, her eyes were red and swollen. She'd run out of tears and decided she needed some good old-fashioned advice, and the one person who could provide that was Josephine Hawks. Cold compresses had reduced the swelling around her eyes, and a hot shower had revitalized her to the point that she felt somewhat human again. But the pain slicing through her heart would need more than compresses and a shower to ease it.

I can't do it.

Those were Hunter's final words before he walked out, and they had spoken volumes. No matter how he felt about her, the responsibility of a family was just not something he wanted in his life, and it seemed he was willing to do anything, including throwing away their relationship, to avoid it. Nothing she could say or do would change that. Even talking to Granny Jo wouldn't change it.

She pulled the car to the side of the road and stopped. So why was she going to the woman's house? Mainly because Granny was really the only friend she'd made in Carson. But why else was she on her way up the mountain? To cry on Granny's shoulder? To see if she had some magical fix for this that would alter Hunter's thinking?

Who was she kidding? There was no magical cure. No one could change how Hunter felt, not even the wise Granny Jo Hawks.

Quickly, she put the car in drive and did a U-turn and then headed back down the mountain. As she drove, she thought about how much Beth and her husband had wanted these children. If only Hunter could want them even a fraction as much. If only she could talk to her friend. Beth always knew what to do, always had the solution to any problem they'd faced.

Then an idea struck her. She could go to Beth's old house and maybe just being there would help her sort through her dilemma. Rose racked her brain to recall the name of the road Beth had lived on. Shawnee. Shantee. Santee Ridge. The first house on the right on Santee Ridge Road. Rose had seen that road sign on her way up the mountain.

She slowed the car and started methodically reading every sign she passed until she found Santee Ridge Road. She swung the car onto the side road and craned her neck searching for the first house.

Then it appeared. A ghostly shell of what had once been a home. She pulled into the driveway and stared at the dilapidated building before her. The rusted mailbox nearly buried in tall weeds held one letter, an *L. L* for Lawrence. Could this be the house Beth had talked about late at night, recounting stories of a happy, wonderful childhood?

If so, where was the picket fence, the yellow roses, the tire swing hanging from the maple tree? Time would have definitely taken a toll on an uninhabited house, but there should have been some trace of the things Beth had described to her. A bit of rotted rope hanging from the tree limb. A remnant of the picket fence. The dried-up stub of a neglected rose bush. Something. But there was nothing. Rose felt as though she'd taken a hard blow to the stomach.

All those stories Beth had told her late at night in whispered confidence. All the dreams they'd dreamed together about Beth getting married and coming back here to raise a family in that happy home where she'd grown up. All so much smoke. Rose leaned back against the car seat, unable to understand any of this.

"Why, Beth? Why did you tell me all that if it wasn't true?" The words emerged like the plaintive cry of a wounded animal.

If Hunter had broken her heart, Beth's manufactured, idyllic life had crushed it. Beth's house of cards, an elaborate charade to protect a little girl from a past she couldn't face, came tumbling down around Rose now. There had never been the perfect life in Carson that Beth had described to Rose. Not then and not now. Not for Beth and not for Rose.

Tears welled in Rose's eyes, but she angrily blinked them away, determined not to waste one more bit of emotion on either Beth or Hunter. They were just one more disappointment added to the parade of disappointments that dotted her life, one more betrayal. She never should have come here. She never should have come to Carson.

Nothing remained for her here. Nothing. Now, it was just her and her babies.

Backing the car out of the driveway, she traveled back down the mountain. Thanks to not having to pay rent, she'd been able to get her car fixed so it was reliable and still stash away enough money to get a small apartment in Charleston and survive for a few weeks while she looked for work.

She laid her hand on her rounded tummy. The best thing she could do for all of them would be to leave Carson behind and begin a new life.

Rose had just thrown the last of her belongings into her car when she heard a vehicle approaching. Taking a deep breath and muttering a quick prayer that it wasn't Hunter, she turned. Lydia's car pulled up beside her.

Davy's mom got out and handed her a large, white envelope. "For you."

She took it and glanced from it to Lydia. "What's this?"

Lydia smiled. "Open it."

Rose slid her finger beneath the flap and

pulled out the single, slick sheet inside. Her breath caught in her throat. Staring back at her from the color, glossy print was her and Hunter huddled together, laughing. Hunter had his arm slung casually around her shoulders. Rose knew exactly when the photo had been taken. They'd been watching Rosebud chase George up the tree.

"Thanks." To her horror, emotion clogged her voice. Though she'd been sure her already bruised heart couldn't hurt anymore, it did. She quickly cleared her throat. "This is very nice of you."

Lydia laughed. "Well, after seeing the two of you together, I figured you'd like it."

"Yes . . . uh . . . I'll just tuck it away for now and get it framed later." She slipped the photo back into the envelope and then dropped it through the window onto the passenger seat of the car. "How's Davy?"

"Better, but not himself. It helped that the man from the wolf preservation place called this morning to tell him that Sadie got there safely, and that they'd turned her loose to run with a pack that they thought she'd acclimate to."

"That was nice of him. He didn't have to do that."

"No, he didn't, and he told me before he talked to Davy that he'd like me to bring

Davy up there so he could see how the animals were treated. Maybe even see Sadie if she's around." She leaned her hip against the fender as though settling in for a long chat.

Rose only half heard her. She was too busy hoping Lydia would leave so she could get out of here before Hunter came back. But she felt compelled to comment. "That would be great for Davy. Put his mind at ease."

"I'm not sure anything is going to do that. He really misses that animal. He didn't eat breakfast this morning, which is unlike him." She pushed herself away from the car and rested her hand on the door handle. "Well, I have to get home. I'm cooking supper for Ken tonight." She flushed a faint pink.

Rose glanced nervously down the driveway. She wanted to wish Lydia luck with Ken, but she didn't say anything because it might signal Lydia that she wanted to lengthen their conversation. Besides, talking about someone else's happy relationship when she had no hope for one herself wasn't what Rose wanted right now.

"Well, you two have fun. Tell Davy hi for me."

Lydia seemed to take the hint that the

conversation was over. She nodded, then threw Rose a questioning look. "You okay?"

Rose forced a smile. "Never better."

"You sure?"

"Yes, I'm sure." She took the car's door handle from Lydia and opened it for her. "Now, get out of here. You've got a meal to cook for a special guy."

Lydia cast one more skeptical look Rose's way, then got in, started the car, waved and drove away.

Rose watched her go, envy growing inside her like a debilitating virus. What she wouldn't give to have what Lydia had.

Hunter sat in Terri's Tearoom doodling random circles on a napkin with the tip of his finger and staring blankly out the window at Main Street. It had been two days since he'd come home and found Rose's car gone. Assuming she'd needed some space to think, he'd shrugged it off and went to bed. But when she hadn't returned by the next morning or that afternoon, he knew in his heart that she was gone for good.

Since then he hadn't been any good to himself or his business. He'd fed and watered the animals and treated the dogs and cats in his care, but he hadn't answered the phone. The red light on the answering

241

machine had been blinking for two days, and he had no desire to hear any of the messages. However, he'd listened to them, just in case one message might be from Rose. But none of them had been, and those were the only ones he'd want to hear.

He sighed, crumpled the napkin and looked out the window.

Oblivious to the pain of the man staring out at the people passing by the window, life went on as usual on Main Street. Sam Watkins hurried down the street, stopping periodically to hand bundles of mail to the store owners. Bill Keeler was hanging a Buy One, Get One Free sign in the market window. Reverend Thomas had just inserted an *s* in the sign on the church lawn announcing his topic for Sunday's sermon, "Moving Mountains." Bessie Wright busied herself pulling weeds out of the petunias in the town square. Several kids stood outside Bart Lawson's bicycle shop eyeing the newest bike parked out front.

None of them knew that Hunter's heart was breaking. None of them realized that he'd stupidly chased away the one woman in the world that he'd ever loved. And more than likely, none of them cared. They had their own lives, their own problems.

He sipped his lukewarm coffee and rearranged the crumbs on his plate that were left from a cheese Danish he hadn't tasted, but had eaten anyway.

He had no idea where Rose had gone, and even if he did, how could he repair the damage he'd done by walking out on her without explanation? How did he explain that her news about her pregnancy had been too much for him to handle on top of everything else that had gone on that day?

"Where have you been?"

Hunter looked up to see his brother Ken standing beside the table. The grim expression on his brother's face told Hunter he was not happy with him. Ken slipped into the chair across from him, rested his folded arms on the table and leaned forward.

"I've been calling you for two days."

Hunter had heard Ken's messages, but dismissed them along with the rest. "I haven't been answering the phone."

"No kidding?" Ken's sarcastic reply held barely controlled irritation. "What's going on, Bro? Talk to me."

Feeling like a jerk, but needing someone to talk to more than needing to protect his ego, Hunter told Ken everything from his love for Rose to his exit after her announcement about the twins. "I really messed up."

"Yes, you did."

"You could at least argue with me." He gave Ken a weary smile.

"I'm not going to stroke your ego so you can justify hurting that great gal. She needed you, and you walked away from her." Ken's irritation had turned to anger. "Why?"

Hunter shook his head and combed his fingers through his already disheveled hair. "I don't know, Ken. A family? All that responsibility? I'm not sure I'm up to facing that again."

Ken laughed, but the sound held no humor. "Who do you think you are? Somebody special? Life is a responsibility. Your animals are as much of a responsibility as any gaggle of kids. The only difference is that their bodies are covered with fur and they can't sass you back."

"I know, but raising you guys was so much harder than taking care of the animals."

"And you did it . . . alone. Something tells me if you have Rose by your side, it's not going to be that hard. The burden won't be as weighty."

"But she's gone. She left."

Ken made an exasperated sound. "What did you expect her to do? Hang around and wait for you to get your head together? You need to find her and talk to her."

Hunter signaled the waitress for two cups of coffee. "That's easier said than done. I have no idea where she went."

"Does she have family?"

Hunter shook his head. "She was abandoned by her mother. Grew up in foster homes. The person closest to her died in a car accident. That's who she was carrying the babies for as a surrogate. She has no one that I know of."

"She did have someone."

Hunter stared at Ken. "Who?"

"You."

"Big help I was."

The waitress arrived with a fresh cup of coffee for Ken and refilled Hunter's. Ken gave her a few bills and waved her off. "Maybe I can find her. I have some connections."

Hunter stared down at the curls of steam wafting from the hot coffee. He had never felt so defeated in his life. Not even when he was raising Janice and Ken, and the money had gotten so sparse he hadn't been sure where their next meal was coming from.

But you did it. You raised two wonderful human beings to adulthood and helped them establish good careers. You did it alone and against all odds. It's about time you stopped feeling sorry for yourself and realize that life doesn't come with guarantees and responsibility is a part of it. Look around you. Everyone has some kind of burden to carry through life.

It suddenly occurred to him that Ken was right. He'd seen something Hunter had been blinded to. Since Rose had come on the scene, she'd shared his responsibilities at the clinic. She'd never been just a receptionist/nurse. She'd fielded George's incessant tirades about the animals, went up against him when he mistreated Davy, and hatched an idea to try to save the wild animals, and all without asking Hunter to help. That wasn't the kind of woman who sat back and let her man run the show and shoulder all the burdens. She'd been as close to a partner as possible.

What a blind, stupid fool he'd been. He looked at his brother. "Where do we start?"

Before Ken could say anything, the door to the tearoom swung open, and Sheriff Ainsley strode in. He made his way purposefully toward them and stopped beside their table.

"There's a town council meeting on Friday night, Doc, and you need to be there."

CHAPTER 16

Three days later, on Friday night, Hunter walked into the Carson town council meeting at the town hall. The only empty chair was in the front. The town's citizens packed the rest of the room. As he made his way toward the front, people called out to him, smiled at him, shook his hand and assured him they were on his side.

His side? For what?

Baffled, he took his seat and waited for whatever it was that was going to happen to begin.

A few minutes later, the three-member Council filed in and sat behind the long table at the front of the room, facing the assembled crowd. In the middle, a smug smile plastered on his face, was George Collins. To his right, Asa Watkins, the president of the Carson Savings and Loan and school superintendent, fiddled with a pen and avoided eye contact with Hunter. To the mayor's left, Catherine Daniels, the town's matriarch, shuffled the papers in front of her, her enormous diamond ring reflecting the glow from the fluorescent ceiling lights.

Sheriff Ben Ainsley stood sentinel just inside the door leading to the hall. He smiled at Hunter and winked. The gesture confused Hunter. Everyone was acting weird tonight. What the heck was going on?

When Collins pounded the oak gavel on the table, Hunter jumped out of his thoughts. "The meeting of the Carson Town Council will come to order." Collins flashed what Rose referred to as his *smarmy smile* at the gathering. "It's nice to see so many of our citizens attending this evening."

A murmur of whispers floated through the crowd. George pounded the gavel again. Hunter got the feeling that since his election, George and the gavel had become one entity. Obviously, slamming it against the table and reigning over the council meetings was another of his mayoral duties that George thoroughly enjoyed.

"The first order of business is discussion on a motion brought to the floor by Catherine Daniels at the last meeting to install a street light on the corner of Hanover and Elm."

The council immediately launched into a

detailed discussion of the pros and cons of adding the street light. Bessie Wright, who lived two houses down on Hanover, claimed the street was so dark at night and the sidewalk was so uneven that she darn near broke her neck walking her dog a few weeks back. Bill Keeler claimed he'd walked into Charlie Henderson's shrubs because he didn't see them.

Behind him, Hunter heard someone whisper that Bill, a faithful patron of Hannigan's Bar out on Route 7, was probably too drunk to see the hedges. Several snickers followed. George banged his gavel again and glared at the offenders. More discussion followed. Finally the council decided unanimously to install the street light, but only after Catherine Daniels said she'd foot the cost of buying and installing it.

Hunter didn't hear what the next topic to be debated was. He'd tuned them out while he tried to figure out what was so important that Ainsley felt the town's veterinarian had to be at this meeting when he could be out with Ken looking for Rose. Hunter had just made up his mind to slip out as unobtrusively as possible when Collins called for new business.

Sam Watkins, the mailman, farmer and Asa's older brother — more his opposite than any man in the room — stepped up to a small podium, which had been provided for the public to address the council, at the side of the council table.

"Sam, what can we do for you?" George favored the older man with his best saccharin smile.

"I'll tell you what you can do. I don't know how you hornswoggled these folks," he waved his hand to take in the other two members, "to go along with you. Although I have my suspicions." He stared straight at his brother. "But you need to let Doc Mackenzie keep his wild animal refuge." Sam crossed his arms defiantly and glared at George.

A bit of color drained from the mayor's face. Obviously he'd not been expecting this.

Hunter perked up. So this was why Ben Ainsley wanted him here. But what good could it possibly do to bring this up now. The animals were gone.

"Furthermore, we want you to get all his animals back. The ones you took away the other day are not dangerous. They're hurt, and there ain't nobody better at fixing hurt animals than Doc. He saved my prize mare Matilda when she had colic, and I know he's saved a lot of other animals." A roar of agreement went up from the crowd. Sam smacked the podium with the palm of his hand. "That's all I have to say."

No sooner had he stepped away than Granny Jo Hawks took his place. "I go along with what Sam said one hundred percent. Those animals are mostly like puppies that sleep and eat all the time, and the ones that aren't, are usually injured and not gonna hurt anyone. Doc sees to that." She pursed her lips, frowned and pointed an accusatory finger at Collins. "You mark my words, George Collins, that boy of yours is gonna follow in Doc's footsteps. He's a natural with four-legged critters. Just because you don't want him out there with them is no reason to shut Doc down. If you had half a brain in your head, you'd see that. As for little Davy, you broke that little boy's heart when you had them take away his wolf. For God's sake, man, stop being a mayor for a little while and be a father. Don't you have any feelings for your son?"

The room broke into cheers of agreement with Granny Jo.

George had the good grace to look reprimanded. Pink tinted his pale cheeks.

Hunter had heard enough. He'd let Rose fight his battle with George. Now he was allowing the good people of Carson to do it. It was time he stood up for himself.

George pounded his gavel for order. "That wolf was —"

"That wolf was harmless." Hunter's voice rose above the noise of the cheering throng. He stood and went to join Granny at the podium. "Just like all the other animals out there were, just like I've been telling you for weeks. Aside from the fact that most of them aren't old enough to do damage, they were either locked in cages or pens, and the ones that weren't locked up were hurt and incapable of doing harm to anyone."

"What about that wolf? She isn't a baby. And what about that vicious hog that chased after me?" George's complexion had regained its color, and his smug expression told Hunter that he thought he'd made a good argument.

A wave of snickers rolled across the room.

"The hog is barely out her mama's womb and quite harmless. As for the wolf . . . Yes, she's full grown and wild, but she hasn't offered to hurt anyone — your son included. Sadie loves Davy, and he loves her. They became friends instantly, and in all my years as a vet, I have never seen a wild wolf become so attached, placid and affectionate with a human as she was with your son. Granny Jo's exactly right. He's got a touch with animals that can't be denied. It's a gift.

Whether or not you recognize that or whether or not the council allows the wild animals back into the refuge, as long as his mother approves, Davy will have a job at my clinic. So, if you think that closing me down or taking away the animals will keep Davy away, forget it."

Again the cheers erupted. George didn't even try to stop them this time. Catherine Daniels clapped as loud as any of the spectators. Asa Watkins stared at the audience openmouthed, his gaze flicking from the crowd to George, uncertain whom to side with.

In the midst of the uproar, Sheriff Ainsley came running up the middle aisle, the grin on his face nearly splitting it in two. "Doc, you gotta see this. You're not gonna believe it." He turned to Collins. "And you best see it, too."

Hunter followed Ben outside, trailed closely by Granny Jo and the rest of the townspeople. He glanced over his shoulder and saw George elbowing his way through to the front of the crowd. By the time they reached the Town Hall steps, Collins was right next to Hunter.

The crowd expelled a simultaneous gasp and came to an abrupt halt.

"Well, my stars. If that don't beat all,"

Granny Jo murmured.

On the sidewalk, standing side by side like any boy and his pet dog were Davy and Sadie.

The boy grinned at Hunter as if Christmas had come early. For him, it probably had.

"She ran all the way back to me, Doc."

"I see that, Davy."

"Mom called the man at the wolf place to tell him, and he said if she wanted to be here bad enough to travel all that way, he wasn't gonna take her away again. He says he'll come by and check on her once in a while, but she can live with me as long as I let her run free." He squatted down next to Sadie and looped his arm over her back as best he could, then buried his face in her fur. The massive animal craned her neck around and licked his cheek.

Hunter grinned and turned to George. "Well, Collins, does that look like a dangerous animal to you?"

Rose looked around her small, furnished apartment. Not lavish by any stretch of the imagination, but good enough until she could afford something bigger and better, and with the job she'd gotten at the Charleston Medical Center, that shouldn't be too long.

She levered herself onto the fold-out couch, grabbed the TV remote and began channel surfing. When the face of a gray wolf flashed on the screen, she stopped pushing the button. For a while, she watched.

The program showcased a couple who ran a wolf awareness program that took in wolves brought to them and reintroduced them back into the wild, but at the same time tried to educate people about the species.

Finally, when she could stand the memories racing through her head of Davy and Hunter and Sadie no longer, Rose turned off the TV and opted for a book instead. But even a good crime novel didn't have the power to still the memories that clung like attic cobwebs to her conscious mind.

She told herself sternly that dreaming about what was and what could never be would do no good. But it didn't dispel the memories. Putting the book aside, she grabbed the mail.

A square white envelope caught her attention. In the upper left corner was Granny Jo's address — the only person in Carson who knew where Rose had relocated. And she had been sworn to secrecy.

What could this be? She opened the ivory

envelope and slid out the matching card inside and read.

Mrs. Earl Hawks requests the honor of
your presence
At
The wedding of her granddaughter
Rebecca Marie Hawks
And
Nicholas Aaron Hart
On Saturday, August Twenty-Seventh . . .

Rose stopped reading. A wedding. How could she possibly attend a wedding when her own dreams of a family and a future lay in dust? Just reading the invitation made her heart hurt. She started to lay the invitation aside when she noticed a small piece of paper hanging from the envelope. Slipping it out, she unfolded it and read.

Dear Rose,
    I know you're probably wondering why on earth I'm sending you an invitation to come back here. To put it simply, we miss you . . . ALL of us. Besides that, there's something you need to see for yourself.

Love, Granny Jo

Rose laid the note aside. Something she

needed to see for herself? What could Granny possibly be talking about? And what did she mean by ALL of us? Did that include Hunter? Did he miss her as much as she missed him? Or was that just Granny's way of saying the townspeople who had brought their animals to the clinic missed her?

Well, whatever it was, Rose was not going back there to find out. The pain was still too fresh, the wounds to her heart too raw. She'd made her break and going back would just resurrect the old hurts, and she was not about to do that.

Besides, in four months she'd have more than enough to help her forget. More importantly, right now the babies came first, and getting into more of an emotional tangle than she was already in certainly couldn't be good for them. She was better off staying out of Carson and away from everything there.

She dropped the invitation in the trash.

CHAPTER 17

Rose looked hesitantly at the invitation in the wastebasket. Could she really not go to Becky's wedding? Rose had never met Becky, so there was no tug of friendship making her second-guess her decision. But there was Granny Jo. Wouldn't she in essence be snubbing Granny Jo if she stayed away? The old woman had been a good friend when Rose needed one. Could she intentionally hurt Granny that way?

Pulling the invitation from the trash, Rose sat down on the couch, the envelope clutched in her hand, indecision clawing at her mind. Go. Don't go. Standing, she went to the window and gazed out on the gray streets of Charleston, the tall buildings that blocked out the sun, the lack of trees and other greenery, the people who passed by without even a nod of greeting. Her heart ached for the beautiful serenity of Hawks Mountain and the cheery friendliness of the people of Carson.

But could she go back? It was a long drive, and she wasn't sure her car would make it. August was one of the hottest months of the year, and the drive would be grueling in her condition.

You're making lame excuses, she told herself. *Your car's been fixed, and it made it here. It can most assuredly make it back there. And you have air-conditioning in the car so the August heat is a moot point. You don't have to interact with anyone. Simply go to the ceremony, wish the bride and groom good luck, give them your gift and then come home. If you don't go you won't find out what it is Granny Jo said you needed to see.*

Now that all her excuses had gone up in smoke, she could be honest with herself. Truth be told, she was afraid of seeing Hunter, afraid that even being in the same building with him would give rise to the pain of losing him all over again. She'd worked very hard establishing a new life, a life free of him. How could she destroy all that?

Despite her misgivings about attending the wedding, the morning of August twenty-seventh, she'd pawed through her closet for something that still fit over her now protruding middle, found a blue dress with an Empire waist whose style complimented her growing body and whose color accentuated her eyes. Then, after prolonged primping and getting her hair just so and her makeup perfect, she'd driven north knowing that coming to this event had the distinct potential to open wounds that had barely begun to heal.

The day dawned warm, sunny and as bright as a new penny. Rose stepped over the threshold of St. Paul's Church. The sanctuary looked as if someone had scooped up Mother Nature and moved her inside. Huge satin bows hung from the end of every pew. The perfume from the yellow carnations and white daisies, overflowing from large vases that adorned the altar and each sill below the stained glass windows, filled the air. The residents of Carson filled all the pews to capacity. Rose wondered if there was anyone in town who hadn't been invited to share the joining of Rebecca Hawks and Nicholas Hart.

Suddenly, she became conscious of being stared at. Several faces had turned toward her. Some familiar ones flashed smiles of recognition. Some held curiosity. She took a hesitant step backward. She could still leave. It wasn't too late.

"Ma'am." The voice beside her stirred Rose out of her thoughts. A handsome young man she recognized at Jeb Tanner, the star quarterback of the high school football team, held out his arm to her. Today he didn't look like a football player. His shoulder pads and jersey had been replaced by a tux that fit him like a glove, and he looked older than his seventeen or eighteen years. "May I escort you to your seat?"

Rose nodded, then linked her arm with his and started down the aisle. Her tangled nerves resembled the embroidery threads at the bottom of one of her foster mother's sewing baskets. Gathering her threatening emotions into a tight ball, she stared straight ahead, making a concentrated effort not to search the faces for the one she wanted to see, but at the same time dreaded seeing most.

"Rose." The stage whisper had come from somewhere to her right.

Rose turned toward it to find Lydia smiling at her and motioning for her to take the empty seat beside her.

"I'll sit here," Rose told the young man. He stood aside while she slid into the seat, then turned and went back to the door to wait for the next guest he would escort in. She peered to Lydia's other side. "Where's

Davy and Ken?"

"Ken took Davy fishing. Davy didn't seem too interested in attending a wedding. He said weddings are for girls." She laughed softly. "So Ken suggested he stay home with him, and that they do something *manly* instead. I let them off the hook." Lydia looked pointedly at Rose's swollen tummy. "When are you due?"

"Two months, but probably sooner. Twins." she said, knowing no further explanation was needed to a woman who was already a mom. Rose dropped her gaze to her hands, avoiding the inevitable follow-up question that Lydia was too polite to ask. Finally, Rose looked at her. Lydia was a good person and definitely not a gossip. Not telling her seemed foolish. "They're not Hunter's."

"Oh," was all Lydia said, but the one word held a lot of surprise and a million more questions.

Briefly, Rose explained about Beth, then added, "I hadn't planned on being a mom and I'm not sure I can be one, but it seems I don't have much say in the matter now that Beth's gone."

Lydia patted her hand and leaned closer. "You'll do fine. It all comes naturally. There will be stumbling blocks, but you'll get past them. Besides, Hunter will come to his senses and be there to help, won't he?"

That Lydia knew about the situation between Rose and Hunter didn't surprise her. Ken had probably confided in her and besides that, in small towns like Carson, gossip traveled faster than a swarm of locusts in a wheat field. Despite all that, Rose wanted to set the record straight about her and Hunter. She opened her mouth to tell Lydia, but the organ music stopped any further conversation.

The young man who had escorted Rose brought Granny Jo down the aisle to the front. The older woman looked stunning. Her hair had obviously been done by a beautician, and the muted-yellow, lace dress she wore suited her to a *T*. A small corsage of daisies lay against her shoulder. As she passed Rose, she winked and smiled at her.

Shortly after Granny Jo was seated, the wedding march began to play, and the usual wedding parade of a maid of honor, two bridesmaids, and a ring bearer made their way up the aisle. Then came a flower girl dispersing silk rose petals over the wooden floor. Becky followed in her wake in a flowing gown of white lace, bugle beads and glittering sequins. In her hands she held a large bouquet of daisies and yellow carnations with a white ribbon cascading to the floor.

When Becky passed her and Rose turned forward, she found that a very handsome, tuxedo-clad Nicholas Hart stood in front of the altar with his groomsmen watching his bride approach. A smile that rivaled the summer sun lit his face. He took her hand, and Reverend Thomas began speaking.

"Dearly beloved . . ."

The beautiful ceremony, complete with vows written by the bride and groom, took Rose's breath away. They looked so much in love, as if nothing in this world existed at that moment but each other.

Tears stung her eyes. These two beautiful people had a future to look forward to while all she had was the uncertainty of motherhood. Coming here had been a huge mistake. It had only served as a raw reminder of all the things she'd never have with Hunter.

How she wished . . . She stopped that thought before it could fully form. No sense wishing for things that could never be.

From his seat at the very back of the church, Hunter had seen Rose come in. And he hadn't been able to take his eyes off her ever since. He didn't need to be next to her to know that the color of her dress matched the sky blue of her eyes or that touching her skin would be like caressing a rose petal or that her hair smelled like mountain wild-flowers. He'd stored all that away in his memory and only took it out when the pain of having lost her became unbearable.

The months since Rose had left had been the longest months of his life, and her appearance here came as a shock to Hunter. A pleasant one, but nevertheless a shock.

Ken had employed every asset at his disposal to find her, but no one seemed to know where she'd gone. Still, he hadn't given up hope that either she'd turn up or they'd get a break and locate her. But he'd never in a million years expected her to come walking into the church as though she'd been here all along.

Hunter had been so focused in on Rose that he hadn't heard one word of the ceremony. When the organ blasted out the strains of "We've Only Just Begun," he jumped, surprised to find the bride and groom walking out the door arm in arm, followed by the wedding party, then a grinning Granny Jo.

As the guests began to file out, he watched Rose make her way down the aisle and thought about approaching her, asking her to walk with him so he could explain his abrupt departure when she told him about the babies. Maybe even take her to the reception at the church hall.

The she looked up. Their gazes locked. She blinked, frowned, shook her head and then looked quickly away and hurried out the door. Hunter's heart sank. Obviously she didn't want to talk to him.

He sat there for a long time as the church emptied out and the guests greeted the newlyweds at the door. He had no desire to interact with anyone — least of all a happy couple embarking on a life of love and happiness together.

Outside the church doors, Rose paused and let the summer sun take the chill from her body. Seeing Hunter had drained all the warmth from her. She'd hoped he would make some move to speak to her, but when he just stared, she knew that hope was futile.

Mechanically, she filed with the other guests past the bridal party, saying the right thing, wishing them happiness when her own heart lay in shattered bits inside her, and wanting it to be over so she could go back to her tiny apartment and cry.

Just beyond the milling crowd, she caught sight of Ken and Davy waiting for Lydia. Forcing a smile she didn't feel, she walked toward them.

"Hey, Miss Rose," Davy called, smiling and waving. Then he paused and stared pointedly at her belly. "Wow, you sure did get fat!"

"Davy!" Lydia grabbed his arm. "That's not polite. Apologize."

His gaze dropped to his feet. "Sorry."

"I'll forgive you if you tell me all about Sadie." Anything to keep from thinking about Hunter.

The changed expression on the boy's face rivaled the sun. "Sadie's gonna be a mom! Isn't that cool, Miss Rose?"

"A mom?" She glanced at Lydia, who nodded. "Well, that's terrific. You're gonna have a whole bunch of wolves to take care of now."

"Yeah. Doc says it's not usual for wolves to get pregnant this time of year. He thinks she'll have five or six pups."

"And when is this going to happen?"

"In a couple of months. We'll be taking her out to the Doc's place when she gets close to having them, so she doesn't wander off in the woods. Last time, somebody killed all her babies."

Rose gasped. "How did you know that?"

The boy bit his lip. "I heard you and Doc talking one time."

Ken laid his hand on Davy's shoulder. "Hey, sport. How about you wait in the car for your mom and me? I wanna talk to Miss Rose for a minute."

"Okay. Bye, Miss Rose." He scampered off toward the parking lot.

"Bye, Davy." She watched him for a moment, and then turned to Ken. His smile did nothing to calm the butterflies that had suddenly erupted in her stomach. She had a feeling she knew what Ken wanted to talk about, but asked anyway. "What did you want to talk to me about?"

Chapter 18

"Actually," Ken said, looking very secretive, but also pleased, "I didn't want to talk to you so much as to show you something." He glanced away from Rose for a second to follow Davy. Rose presumed it was to make sure he was going to the car and not wandering off.

Rose hesitated. "What is it that you want to show me?"

"Go with him, child." Granny Jo had come to stand beside them in the church parking lot. "You need to see this."

Still Rose hesitated. Was this what Granny had said in her note that Rose needed to see? "What is it I need to see and where are we going?"

Rose glanced from Ken to Granny Jo and then to Lydia. All of them were looking at her with toothy grins that should have been center stage in a toothpaste ad. Obviously this was something the three of them had concocted amongst themselves.

The older woman smiled. "You'll see. Now, go along with Ken." She placed her hand in the small of Rose's back and gave her a gentle nudge forward toward the car where Davy was grinning at her through the back window.

Still unsure of what to do, she played for time and glanced around the empty church parking lot. All the wedding guests had gone to the reception. The only vehicles left were Ken's and that of an older woman beckoning frantically for Granny Jo to join her.

"I'm coming," Granny Jo called to her friend, then kissed Rose's cheek and hurried off.

Rose turned to her companions. Still stalling for time, she asked Lydia and Ken, "What about the reception? Don't you two want to go, too?"

Lydia linked her arm with Rose's. "We'll catch up with them later." Gently, she propelled Rose toward their car. "Now, come on. This is more important."

Still a bit uncertain, Rose walked with Lydia to the car and climbed into the backseat beside Davy. She leaned over and whispered, "Where are we going?"

Davy shook his head, and then placed a finger over his lips. "It's a secret. But you're gonna like it."

"Davy," his mother warned sternly from the front seat. "Zip your lip."

He made a motion across his mouth as if pulling a zipper closed. Evidently Rose wasn't going to get anyone to talk. Resigning herself to taking this mystery ride, she leaned back in the seat.

Ken guided the car out of the church parking lot and headed out of town and then onto Lower Mountain Road. As they drove up the winding road, Rose looked out her side window and wracked her brain to figure out what it could possibly be that they were so anxious for her to see, but nothing came to mind. Then she glanced at her fellow occupants of the car. No one was talking, but she could see an extremely pleased grin on Ken's face in the rearview mirror.

She was about to take another stab at getting Davy to talk when Ken made a right hand turn onto Santee Ridge Road. Rose froze. Why were they going up here?

"Ken —"

Before she could finish, Ken had turned the car into the driveway of what had once been Beth's home. But it didn't resemble the ramshackle house Rose had seen on the day she'd left Carson. She blinked, unable

271

to believe what lay before her.

Emotions far too complicated to sort out swirled inside her. Confusion, surprise, puzzlement and a profound sense of delight that someone had brought the house back to life.

Between the road and the freshly mowed lawn stood a white picket fence, obviously new and recently erected. The rusted mailbox had been exchanged for a shiny aluminum one, but there was no name on it to identify the occupants of the house. The house itself had been painted a bright white that glowed in the summer sun. Broken window panes and missing roof shingles had been replaced. The formerly rickety porch appeared to have been totally rebuilt and extended the full length of the front of the house. At one end of the porch, a gentle breeze nudged two rocking chairs into motion, making them appear as if they were occupied by ghosts.

Thinking that someone had bought the house, fixed it up and wanted to sell it, she looked around for a For Sale sign. But there was none. But none of this explained why they'd brought her here.

Then something else caught her attention . . . the profusion of blooming, yellow, summer rose bushes that had been planted at the base of the porch foundation. Exactly where Beth had said they were when she'd lived here, but Rose doubted her friend had ever had lived here, and if she had, it certainly hadn't been anything like Beth had painted it.

Were the roses a coincidence?

Ken turned sideways in his seat and smiled. "Well, what do you think?"

Rose couldn't find her voice. She was too busy sorting through all she'd seen, trying to understand what it had to do with her.

Davy opened his car door and grabbed her hand. "Come on. You have to see what's out back."

Hampered by her protruding belly, Rose climbed clumsily from the backseat, and then followed him up the front path. Ken and Lydia quickly brought up the rear. At the front steps, the path divided into a *Y*. One section led to the house, the other veered around the porch toward the backyard.

Davy took her hand and tugged. "Come on, Miss Rose. Hurry up. This way." He guided her past the porch and around the corner where she stopped dead in her tracks.

Hanging from the old maple tree were two baby swings suspended on chains from heavy-duty eye hooks screwed into the fat limbs. She was beginning to suspect who the new owner was, but it made no sense.

The boy held out a hand in the direction of the tree, as if he was introducing a rock star to a concert audience. "Well . . ."

Rose frowned. "I don't understand."

"Two swings," he said as though she couldn't see them.

"Yes, I can see that, but —"

"One for each of the babies."

Rose stiffened. Her heart began to race. That voice could belong to only one person. Dare she hope?

Slowly she turned around. Davy, Lydia and Ken had moved off to the side of the yard, but Hunter stood a few feet away.

He looked . . . hesitant, maybe even a bit afraid. Nevertheless, she drank in the sight of him. The glimpse she'd had in the church hadn't been nearly enough to fill the empty hole in her heart.

She couldn't recall him being so tanned, or his hair having so many blonde streaks through it. But his eyes . . . oh, those eyes. They still had the power to make her knees go weak. Wait! Blonde streaks. Tanned skin. Had he . . .

"Did you do all this?" She waved her hand at the house.

He nodded. "I bought it a few weeks after

I went to take care of Sam's colicky horse."

Rose frowned. "Why?"

He took several steps closer to her. "Why do you think? I knew what this house meant to you . . . to Beth and the dreams you both had for it. I also knew how disappointed you'd be if you saw it in the shape it was in before I fixed it." He paused for a moment. "But not nearly as disappointed as you must have been in me the day I walked out." He glanced toward Ken, then back to Rose. "I . . . we searched everywhere for you, but you'd vanished. I wanted to explain. Do you have any idea how scared I was when we couldn't find you?"

A breeze blew the scent of his aftershave to her. The smell brought back memories of long nights with him, of the security of his arms and the gentleness of his hands. "Now do you understand why I did it, why I renovated the house?"

"No. I still have no idea." *Say it, Hunter. Please just say it. Tell me you love me. Tell me you want a future with me and my babies.* She held her breath and waited, but the words never came.

Instead, Hunter covered the space between them and grasped her shoulders. "Because I was an idiot. Because I threw away the thing I wanted most in the world.

Because I hope you'll forgive me and give me another chance."

Rose's heart sank. He hadn't said what she longed to hear. He hadn't said he loved her. But most importantly, he hadn't said he wanted a family with her, that he wanted a life with her and her babies. So nothing had changed. Nothing.

She stepped away and turned her back on him to hide the tears that threatened to fall. "Of course, you're forgiven. I've never been one to hold grudges. And I understand your reluctance to take on the responsibility of raising two babies that aren't even yours. That's only natural. I mean, a man shouldn't have to raise babies he didn't father." *Keep talking. If you keep talking he can't . . . Can't what? Walk away? Tell you there can never be anything between you?* "I can easily see —"

Hunter walked around in front of her, grasped her shoulders and pulled her to him and then kissed her into silence. Kissed her like she'd never been kissed in her life, not even by him. Her head spun, and she had to cling to him to maintain her balance. Then without her permission, her arms snaked around his neck.

Hunter felt her surrender along with the simultaneous relief that washed through his tense body. When Ken told him what he had in mind if Rose showed up at the wedding, Hunter wasn't at all sure it would work. But Ken had assured him she wouldn't know anything until they got to the house. He'd been almost certain it wouldn't work and that Rose would want nothing to do with him. But her reaction to his kiss said differently.

He'd hoped it would work, just as, when he'd undertaken fixing the house up, he'd hoped that one day they would share it with the babies she was carrying. But there had been no guarantees. It could have all blown up in his face.

The only thing that had given him any peace of mind, any optimism, any small thread of faith to cling to that there would be a future with Rose, was the memory of their lovemaking. So sweet, so intense. She couldn't have reacted like that if she didn't love him.

Somewhere behind him Hunter became vaguely aware of the sound of laughter and cheering. Slowly, he released Rose's mouth and turned toward the sound. Davy, grinning from ear to ear, Lydia, beaming, and Ken, with an I-told-you-so expression, stood at the corner of the house applauding.

"Do you guys mind if we have a little —"

Rose stiffened in his arms, pulled away and then cried out in pain. "Oh, my God!"

Hunter jerked his attention back to her. Fear shot through him. "Rose?"

She groaned, then bent double, clutching her abdomen. Loosening one hand, she grabbed Hunter's suit jacket in a desperate white-knuckled grip.

Hunter dropped to his knees and peered up into her ashen face, his hands gripping both her shoulders to steady her. "Rose, honey, what is it?"

She grimaced, opened her eyes and peered at him, her expression flooded with alarm. "The . . . babies . . . I . . . think . . . they're . . . coming."

CHAPTER 19

The hospital noises grated on Hunter's nerves like fingernails on a blackboard. Every time he heard the squeak of rubber shoe soles on the polished tiles he jumped and waited for a nurse or doctor to appear. When they didn't his nerves wound that much tighter.

An hour ago, although to him it seemed like four hours ago, a nurse had informed him that because one of the babies was breech, the doctor would be performing a C-section. She said it wouldn't be long, but Hunter had decided she'd been giving him lip-service to calm him down. However, it had only raised his anxiety level several notches.

Unable to sit still, he paced the small waiting room from wall to wall and windows to wall, stopping only periodically to peer down the hall where Rose had been loaded on a gurney and wheeled away almost two hours earlier. But other than the normal functioning activity of a busy hospital, he saw nothing that would tell him what was going on in the operating room where he'd been told they'd taken Rose.

The EMTs hadn't let him ride in the ambulance. Something about a rule they had because he wasn't her relative. Instead of taking the time to argue that he was the closest thing she had to a relative, Hunter, Ken, Davy and Lydia had followed the ambulance in Ken's car to Charleston. They'd dropped Davy off with a friend of Lydia's, and then went straight to the hospital. There had barely been enough time for him to assure Rose that he'd be there when she got out, before EMTs wheeled her away.

Hunter stopped beneath the large, black clock hanging on the pale green waiting room area wall. Its plain face and oversized hands reminded him of the one that had hung on the wall in his third-grade class-room. As back then when he'd been waiting for recess, those immense hands seemed to have stopped moving. Was it even working? Just then, as if to mock his frustration, the larger of the two hands ticked off another minute with a loud *click*.

"What's taking so long? Why aren't they

coming to tell us anything?" Hunter had asked this same question of the other occupants of the room innumerable times during the long, nerve-wracking wait.

"It'll happen when it happens, brother," Ken said. "They'll let you know when they have something to tell you, and asking every two minutes about how long it's taking isn't going to hurry anything up. Except maybe your nervous breakdown."

"He's right. Hunter," Lydia chimed in. She stood. "How about if I go down to the cafeteria and get us all some coffee?"

"Good idea." Ken dug in his pocket and then handed her some bills. "Hunter and I take ours black."

Between Hunter's taut nerves and the sickening antiseptic smell of the hospital, he had doubts about even keeping a cup of coffee down, but he didn't decline. Instead he just nodded and mumbled, "Thanks, Lydia."

She took the bills from Ken, cast a sympathetic look in Hunter's direction, then hurried from the room.

Hunter sat down in one of the vinyl upholstered chairs, picked up a glossy magazine from a nearby side table and absently leafed through it, seeing nothing but a blur of color as the pages ruffled past his line of vision. Tossing the magazine back on the pile, he finger-combed his hair and then stood and began pacing again.

His insides were a knot of raw nerves. Rose had to be okay. The babies had to be okay. *They will be,* he told himself over and over, but it didn't help. She'd been in there so long, and she'd been in so much pain. Did it mean complications or did C-sections always take this long?

The nurse who had admitted Rose walked by, and Hunter quickly followed her to the desk. "Is there any word about Rose Hamilton yet?"

She hit several keys on her computer's keyboard, waited, then consulted something on the monitor and shook her head. "Not yet, sir. It's probably going to be a few more —"

Hunter didn't wait to hear more. He hurried back to the waiting room. Lydia had returned with three containers of coffee. Hunter accepted one and took a sip. It tasted like turpentine. He set it aside and resumed pacing.

Visions of Rose at the house tormented him. She'd looked so defeated after he'd told her why he renovated the house. Why hadn't he told he loved her and that he wanted to be a father to her babies? He sighed. Would there ever come a time when he ceased to act like a jerk around Rose? He'd known what she wanted to hear, so why hadn't he just said it?

Because you're a coward, Mackenzie. Because you were afraid she'd turn away from you. But she didn't, did she? She only turned away when she thought you still didn't want the responsibility of a family. All she wanted were the words, the commitment.

Silently, he promised himself, God and Rose that he'd make that commitment as soon as he could see her and talk to her again. He loved her and wanted to raise the babies with her. She needed to know that, and he needed to tell her. Now, he just prayed he'd get the chance to say it.

The babies weren't due for a month and a half yet. Was that going to cause problems? The doctor had explained to him that twins often come early and that, with all the modern technology and advances in medicine they have now, preemies have a good survival rate — but what about the mother? He'd never said anything about the survival rate of the mothers.

When he thought about the possibility of never getting the chance to tell Rose how he felt, his heart felt as if a big fist had squeezed it. The pain, emotional and physical, nearly doubled him over.

No! He had to stop this. He had to start thinking positive thoughts. Rose would be fine, and so would the twins. And they'd have a wonderful life together. He had to believe that. If he didn't, they'd be admitting him to the psych ward.

Rose opened her eyes then blinked and then quickly closed them against the glare of the fluorescent lights. The familiar smell of a hospital hung in the air. A periodic, rhythmic beeping was the only sound in the room. It took a moment for her to realize it was her own heartbeat she was listening to.

Slowly, she opened her eyes again and looked down at the blankets covering her. Her tummy was flat. The bulge that had held her babies was gone. Panic gripped her insides. She knew the dangers of premature birth, even at seven and a half months.

"Nurse!" The sound emerged from her dry throat as just above a whisper. She felt for the call button and pressed it over and over.

Seconds later a nurse wearing a smock top covered with tiny brown teddy bears, a name badge that read Marsha Evars, and an alarmed expression on her face raced into the room. "Yes, Ms. Hamilton. What is it?" She hurried to Rose's side.

Rose pushed herself to a half-sitting position. She grimaced at the sharp pain that sliced across her abdomen. "My babies. How are they?"

Relief flooded Marsha's face. "Your babies are fine. Both of them are sleeping soundly in an Isolette in the nursery."

Rose gripped the nurse's fingers so tight, the woman cried out. "But are they okay?"

She smiled. "They're fine. They weighed in a little light, but they should gain their weight in no time. They have all the required number of fingers, toes, eyes, noses and limbs. A little small, but no respiratory problems. Just two very healthy babies."

Unsure of what they'd told her after the babies had been born, Rose asked, "They're girls, right?"

"They sure are. Two beautiful little girls." She pushed gently against Rose's shoulder. "Now, just lie back and relax."

Rose resisted. "When can I see them?"

Urging Rose gently, but firmly back against the pillows, Marsha smiled and tucked the sheet in. "As soon as the doctor comes in and gives the okay. Your tummy is gonna be sore for a while so you can't rush into too much movement. Now, you just take it easy. You've had a big day. You'll see your daughters very soon. Promise."

Reassured, Rose relaxed against the pillows. She thought about the two lives she'd just brought into the world. Two little girls. I have two little girls. It dawned on her at that moment that somewhere along the way she'd stopped thinking of the twins as Beth's babies and started thinking of them as hers. Rose's daughters. Maybe she would be good at this mother stuff after all.

Despite her efforts to stay awake, Rose's eyelids drooped. The last thing she recalled was the nurse smiling down at her, and then hurrying from the room.

Hunter stared through the window at the incubators holding the tiny babies Rose had given birth to about an hour before. It was incredible how small they were and hard to imagine that anything that little would one day be going to college and getting married and having babies of her own.

Even more incredible was that Hunter realized exactly how much he wanted to be there to see all of that happen. He wanted to see their first steps, hear their first words, take them to their first day of school, interrogate their first dates, walk each of them down the aisle on his arm on their wedding day. And he wanted to do it all with Rose at his side.

A knock on the glass in front of him roused him from his wishful musings. He recognized the nurse immediately as Cindy Newman. She'd been to his office many times with Herman, a very large, drooling Saint Bernard, who had a penchant for investigating porcupines in a very up close and personal way.

Cindy motioned for him to go to the door to the nursery. He did as she asked. The door swung open. "Hi, Doc."

"Cindy."

"These your babies? Or are you checking them out for a friend?"

How did he answer that? He finally settled on what he hoped would be the case after speaking to Rose. "They're my girlfriend's."

"Well then, how about you come in and get acquainted with them? I'll even let you hold them."

Hunter hesitated. Was he really sure he wanted to do this? He glanced past Cindy to where the pink-skinned, fragile-looking babies lay, hands punching the air. God, they were so tiny, so delicate. He'd never held a baby before, at least not a human baby. What if he hurt one of them?

He took a step backward. "Uh . . . I don't know if that's a good idea."

Cindy smiled. "Sure it is. Come on. They're little but they won't break." She took his arm and led him into a small anteroom where she handed him a set of green scrubs. "Put these on, then come on out and meet your girls." She closed the door.

His girls. Calm contentment infused with warmth and happiness spread through him. It was as if someone had removed every care in the world from his shoulders. He recognized the feeling immediately. It was the same feeling he got when he held Rose in his arms. It was love. But how could he love these tiny lives already?

Quickly, he slipped the scrubs over his street clothes.

"Ready?" Cindy called from the other side of the door.

Hunter opened the door and stepped into the nursery. "Ready." He took a deep breath and followed her to the side of the incubators holding the babies.

"Sit there." Cindy pointed at a rocking chair situated to the side of the room.

He sat and watched as she carefully picked up one of the babies and swathed her in a pink blanket. Then she placed the tiny bundle in his arms. He looked down at her in awe. Only her face was visible, and just looking at her made him feel like he held an angel. Her creamy cheeks held a pink tinge and her blue eyes stared up at him with a mesmerizing intensity that turned his insides to jelly.

"Hello, little one. Do you have any idea how beautiful you are?" He touched her cheek gingerly with his thumb. It felt like silk. Carefully, he pulled back the blanket to see more of her. Before he could put it back in place, she'd wrapped her fingers around his thumb. Hunter's heart swelled until he was afraid it would burst from his chest. Tears choked his throat, but he pushed the words past them. "That's it, sweetheart. You hang on to me because I will always be here for you and your sister. I will make sure that nothing ever hurts either of you and that all you ever know is love and happiness. That's a promise because I'm going to do everything in my power to convince your mom that I should be your dad."

Behind Hunter, Rose let the tears fall freely as she watched him and the baby. She couldn't hear what he was saying, but the look of wonder and love on his face told her more than enough. Maybe there was hope for them as a couple and as a family.

When she could speak, she whispered to

the nurse pushing her wheelchair, "Take me back to my room. I'll see the babies later. I don't want to interrupt that."

The nurse smiled and nodded, turned the chair around and wheeled Rose back to her room, then helped her into the bed.

A half hour later, Hunter stepped into the room. "Hi."

Still unsure of how things lay between them, Rose smiled. "Hi, yourself."

He came to the side of the bed. "Have you seen them yet?"

She shook her head. "Not yet."

His grin lit up the room. "They're beautiful, Rose." Then he laughed and shook his head. "That's such an inadequate word to describe them. They're . . . a miracle . . ." Emotion filled his voice and choked off any further words. He coughed to clear his throat, looking a bit embarrassed at his unbidden display of emotions. "Have you named them?"

"Beth for their mom, and Patricia for their dad, Patrick."

"That's nice. I'm sure Beth and Patrick would be very happy with your choices." Suddenly, he'd become almost formal. Then he started to move away toward the chair at her bedside.

They'd come this far and Rose had no

intentions of allowing him to retreat. She grabbed his hand and pulled him to her, forcing him to sit on the side of the bed. "I need to ask you something."

"What?"

Now it was she who was withdrawing, afraid to admit what she feared most. But if she and Hunter were ever to have a relationship of any kind, they had to stop keeping things from each other. They had to learn to share their burdens, material and emotional. She'd been as guilty of not doing that as he had, and it was time it stopped.

"I've always been afraid that because my mother walked out on me, I wouldn't be a good mom. I remember watching Pansy with her kittens and seeing how instinctively she responded to them." She squeezed his fingers. "I'm scared, Hunter. What if I'm not like Pansy? What if I can't do this?"

He leaned over and kissed her lightly on the mouth. "Remember what I told you when you held that baby lion that first day?"

She shook her head. With the taste of his kiss fresh on her lips, she was having difficulty even thinking, much less remembering anything.

He gently brushed the hair from her cheek. "I said you're a natural, Rose Hamilton. You're a natural with the animals and

291

with Davy, and I have every confidence you'll be a natural with our daughters."

"*Our* daughters?" Fearing she'd heard him wrong, she endeavored to keep the shock and happiness from her voice and failed.

"Yes, our daughters." He kissed her again, this time longer and harder. "I should have said this long ago, but as Granny Jo would say, better late than never. I love you, and I want to marry you and take care of you and those sweet little girls."

Happiness flooded through her like a winter thaw. She could hardly believe her ears. He loved her. He wanted to be a family. She cupped his face in her palms. "I love you, too. All I've ever wanted was for us to be a family."

They kissed again and this time, it sealed a promise and a life together.

Rose pulled away. "Hunter, I lied."

"You what?"

"I lied. I have seen the babies or at least one of them. She was having an intense conversation with you. I didn't want to interrupt. What were you saying to her?"

He laughed and carefully, so as not to hurt her, gathered her in his arms. "I was just telling her what a good dad I'll be, and that I'm gonna love and take care of them and their mom forever."

"Forever?" She gazed up at him and even before he spoke, she saw the promise of his love reflected in his eyes.

Hunter kissed her. "Forever."

Granny's Journal

SUMMER

Hello, y'all!

So nice to see you back in Carson again. I hope you enjoyed your stay.

Well, summer's almost over, and the slight nip in the air, the coloring of the leaves on the big maple out front and the arthritis pain in my knees tells me fall is surely on the way. Now that Nick and Becky's wedding is over, it appears as though things have calmed down in Carson for a time, not that it'll stay that way for long. Never does.

Elections are coming up in a few months, and I have a feeling that George Collins will be retiring as mayor of Carson. What he tried to do to Doc Mackenzie by closing the wildlife refuge didn't win him any votes with the fine people of this community. Added to that mistake is the pain he caused his son Davy by taking away his wolf friend, as a result, he retired from the school board. You should have seen George's face when he saw that the wolf had come back. I swear that animal has more sense than he does.

But that's not all going on hereabouts.

My Becky and Nick are back from their honeymoon in the Caribbean and settled in in his cabin up on the ridge as man and wife, and I couldn't be happier. I can go to my Maker knowing my Becky will be well loved and taken care of and is as happy as a pig in a mud puddle, and it doesn't get much happier than that.

Doc and Rose Mackenzie are living in the old Lawrence place with those beautiful new babies they brought home a while ago. He sure did a fine job fixing that old house up. I get such joy from seeing that man around those babies. He's finding that being a father comes with some pretty special rewards. It's rare that we see him around town without those sweet little girls in tow, and even though Rose doubted her abilities to be a good mama to those babies, they couldn't ask for better. She's a natural at it. But I knew she would be. She's got too much love to give not to be.

Doc's brother Ken seems to be hanging around town a bit longer than he'd planned. I expect that's due to Lydia Collins. The man is in love, though I'm sure he either doesn't know it yet or isn't willing to admit it. It just makes me shake my head in wonder that these young people don't recognize love until it comes up and bites them in the . . . Well, you know. I knew the minute I laid eyes on my Earl that I was in love. Oh well, I guess time will tell. Not sure how Lydia feels. Who can blame her for taking it slow after her bad marriage to George?

The big house south of town that Jonathan Prince is building is coming along nicely. Should be finished in a few months. Just in time for Christmas.

Becky says Mandy, the new girl working for her at the Health and Human Services office in town, is creating quite a stir at the high school. Something about wanting to start a family management class for our teenagers. Somebody needs to. There's far too many of them having to get married because they're in the family way. Word is that Asa Watkins, the superintendent of schools, isn't happy about taking money from the athletic fund to pay for Mandy's idea. The principle, Lucas Michaels, doesn't know which way to turn. Should be some fireworks at the next school board meeting. I told ya that things don't stay quiet around here for long.

Well, I best be getting along. I have to take a couple of quilts over to Rose for those sweet baby girls of theirs.

Come visit us again. Like I always say . . . There's no shortage of excitement around these parts.

Love,
Granny Jo

ABOUT THE AUTHOR

Being a romantic at heart and having devoured romances like Hershey Kisses, it was inevitable that **Elizabeth Sinclair** would one day write them. Following her dream, which took more than a couple of wrong turns along the way, in 1993 she sold her first romance, *Jenny's Castle,* which reached #2 on the Walden Bestseller List and won a Georgia Romance Writers' Maggie Award of Excellence. Since then, this multi-published author's books have sold in ten foreign countries and been translated into seven foreign languages.

Elizabeth is a member of Romance Writers of America, The Author's Guild and Thriller Writers. She's taught creative writing and given seminars and workshops, locally and nationally, on the craft of writing. Her books have finaled in the Daphne de Maurier contest and won The National

Reader's Choice Award, The Anne Bonney Reader's Choice Award, *Romantic Times* Reviewer's Choice Award, the Heart of Excellence Readers Choice Award and earned a Gold Medal Top Pick from the *Romantic Times* Book Club.

Elizabeth co-founded and is a member of the Ancient City Romance Authors of St. Augustine, Florida. She is also a member of RWA's Kiss of Death Chapter, Sisters In Crime, and the Indiana Romance Writers. Elizabeth served as RWA's Region 3 Director and chaired the 2001 RWA New Orleans Annual Conference.

In addition to having authored the widely acclaimed instructional books, *The Dreaded Synopsis* and *First Chapters,* she has published eighteen romances.

Her Hawks Mountain series continues next with *Forever Fall.* Visit her at www .elizabethsinclair.com.